REVENGE OF THE LAWN GNOMES

Look for more Goosebumps books
by R.L. Stine:

Goosebumps

REVENGE OF THE LAWN GNOMES

R. L. STINE

AN
APPLE
PAPERBACK

SCHOLASTIC INC.
New York Toronto London Auckland Sydney

A PARACHUTE PRESS BOOK

ISBN 0-590-48346-3

12 11 10 9 8 7 6 5 4 3 2 1   5 6 7 8 9/9 0/0

Printed in the U.S.A.   40

First Scholastic printing, August 1995

1

Clack, Clack, Clack.

The Ping-Pong ball clattered over the basement floor. "Yes!" I cried as I watched Mindy chase after it.

It was a hot, sticky June afternoon. The first Monday of summer vacation. And Joe Burton had just made another excellent shot.

That's me. Joe Burton. I'm twelve. And there is nothing I love better than slamming the ball in my older sister's face and making her chase after it.

I'm not a bad sport. I just like to show Mindy that she's not as great as she thinks she is.

You might guess that Mindy and I do not always agree on things. The fact is, I'm really not like anyone else in my family.

Mindy, Mom, and Dad are all blond, skinny, and tall. I have brown hair. And I'm kind of pudgy and short. Mom says I haven't had my growth spurt yet.

So I'm a shrimp. And it's hard for me to see over the Ping-Pong net. But I can still beat Mindy with one hand tied behind my back.

As much as I love to win, Mindy hates to lose. And she doesn't play fair at all. Every time I make a great move, she says it doesn't count.

"Joe, *kicking* the ball over the net is not legal," she whined as she scooped out the ball from under the couch.

"Give me a break!" I cried. "All the Ping-Pong champions do it. They call it the Soccer Slam."

Mindy rolled her huge green eyes. "Oh, puh-lease!" she muttered. "My serve."

Mindy is weird. She's probably the weirdest fourteen-year-old in town.

Why? I'll tell you why.

Take her room. Mindy arranges all her books in alphabetical order — by author. Do you believe it?

And she fills out a card for each one. She files them in the top drawer of her desk. Her own private card catalog.

If she could, she'd probably cut the tops off the books so they'd be all the same size.

She is *so* organized. Her closet is organized by color. All the reds come first. Then the oranges. Then the yellows. Then come the greens, blues, and purples. She hangs her clothes in the same order as the rainbow.

And at dinner, she eats around her plate clockwise. Really! I've watched her. First her mashed potatoes. Then all her peas. And then her meat loaf. If she finds one pea in her mashed potatoes, she totally loses it!

Weird. Really weird.

Me? I'm not organized. I'm cool. I'm not serious like my sister. I can be pretty funny. My friends think I'm a riot. Everyone does. Except Mindy.

"Come on, serve already," I called out. "Before the end of the century."

Mindy stood on her side of the table, carefully lining up her shot. She stands in exactly the same place every time. With her feet exactly the same space apart. Her footprints are worn into the carpet.

"Ten–eight and serving," Mindy finally called out. She always calls out the score before she serves. Then she swung her arm back.

I held the paddle up to my mouth like a microphone. "She pulls her arm back," I announced. "The crowd is hushed. It's a tense moment."

"Joe, stop acting like a jerk," she snapped. "I have to concentrate."

I love pretending I'm a sports announcer. It drives Mindy nuts.

Mindy pulled her arm back again. She tossed the Ping-Pong ball up into the air. And . . .

"A spider!" I screamed. "On your shoulder!"

"Yaaaiiii!" Mindy dropped the paddle and began slapping her shoulder furiously. The ball clattered onto the table.

"Gotcha!" I cried. "My point."

"No way!" Mindy shouted angrily. "You're just a cheater, Joe." She smoothed the shoulders of her pink T-shirt carefully. She picked up the ball and swatted it over the net.

"At least I'm a *funny* cheater!" I replied. I twirled around in a complete circle and belted the ball. It bounced once on my side before sailing over the net.

"Foul," Mindy announced. "You're always fouling."

I waved my paddle at her. "Get a life," I said. "It's a game. It's supposed to be fun."

"I'm beating you," Mindy replied. "That's fun."

I shrugged. "Who cares? Winning isn't everything."

"Where did you read that?" she asked. "In a bubble gum comic?" Then she rolled her eyes again. I think someday her eyes are going to roll right out of her head!

I rolled my eyes, too — back into my head until only the whites showed. "Neat trick, huh?"

"Cute, Joe," Mindy muttered. "Really cute. You'd better watch out. One day your eyes might not come back down. Which would be an improvement!"

"Lame joke," I replied. "Very lame."

Mindy lined up her feet carefully again.

"She's in her serve position," I spoke into my paddle. "She's nervous. She's . . ."

"Joe!" Mindy whined. "Quit it!"

She tossed the Ping-Pong ball into the air. She swung the paddle, and —

"Gross!" I shouted. "What's that big green glob hanging out of your nose?"

Mindy ignored me this time. She tapped the ball over the net.

I dove forward and whacked it with the tip of my paddle. It spun high over the net and landed in the corner of the basement. Between the washing machine and the dryer.

Mindy jogged after the ball on her long, thin legs. "Hey, where's Buster?" she called out. "Wasn't he sleeping next to the dryer?"

Buster is our dog. A giant black Rottweiler with a head the size of a basketball. He loves snoozing on the old sleeping bag we keep in the corner of the basement. Especially when we're down here playing Ping-Pong.

Everyone is afraid of Buster. For about three seconds. Then he starts licking them with his long, wet tongue. Or rolls onto his back and begs to have his belly scratched.

"Where is he, Joe?" Mindy bit her lip.

"He's around here somewhere," I replied. "Why

are you always worrying about Buster? He weighs over a hundred pounds. He can take care of himself."

Mindy frowned. "Not if Mr. McCall catches him. Remember what he said the last time Buster chomped on his tomato plants?"

Mr. McCall is our next-door neighbor. Buster loves the McCalls' yard. He likes to nap under their huge, shady elm tree.

And dig little holes all over their lawn. And sometimes big holes.

And snack in their vegetable garden.

Last year, Buster dug up every head of Mr. McCall's lettuce. And ate his biggest zucchini plant for dessert.

I guess that's why Mr. McCall hates Buster. He said the next time he catches him in his garden, he's going to turn him into fertilizer.

My dad and Mr. McCall are the two best gardeners in town. They're nuts about gardening. Totally nuts.

I think working in a garden is kind of fun, too. But I don't let that get around. My friends think gardening is for nerds.

Dad and Mr. McCall are always battling it out at the annual garden show. Mr. McCall usually takes first place. But last year, Dad and I won the blue ribbon for our tomatoes.

That drove Mr. McCall crazy. When Dad's name

was announced, Mr. McCall's face turned as red as our tomatoes.

So Mr. McCall is desperate to win this year. He started stocking up on plant food and bug spray months ago.

And he planted something that nobody else in North Bay grows. Strange orange-green melons called casabas.

Dad says that Mr. McCall has made a big mistake. He says the casabas will never grow any bigger than tennis balls. The growing season in Minnesota is too short.

"McCall's garden loses," I declared. "Our tomatoes are definitely going to win again this year. And thanks to my special soil, they'll grow as big as beach balls!"

"So will your head," Mindy shot back.

I stuck out my tongue and crossed my eyes. It seemed like a good reply.

"Whose serve is it?" I asked. Mindy was taking so long, I lost track.

"It's still my serve," she replied, carefully placing her feet.

We were interrupted by footsteps. Heavy, booming footsteps on the stairs behind Mindy.

"Who is that?" Mindy cried.

And then he appeared behind her. And my eyes nearly bulged right out of my head.

"Oh, no!" I screamed. "It's . . . McCall!"

2

"Joe!" he roared. The floor shook as he stomped toward Mindy.

All the color drained from Mindy's face. Her hand grasped her paddle so tightly that her knuckles turned white. She tried to swing around to look behind her, but she couldn't. Her feet were frozen in her Ping-Pong-ball footprints.

McCall's hands balled into two huge fists, and he looked really, really angry.

"I'm going to get you. And this time I'm going to win. Throw me a paddle."

"You jerk!" Mindy sputtered. "I-I knew it wasn't *Mr.* McCall. I knew it was Moose."

Moose is Mr. McCall's son and my best friend. His real name is Michael, but everyone calls him Moose. Even his parents.

Moose is the biggest kid in the whole sixth grade. And the strongest. His legs are as thick as tree trunks. And so is his neck. And he's very, very loud. Just like his dad.

Mindy can't stand Moose. She says he's a gross slob.

I think he's cool.

"Yo, Joe!" Moose bellowed. "Where's my paddle?" His big arm muscles bulged as he reached out to grab mine.

I pulled my hand back. But his beefy hand slapped my shoulder so hard that my head nearly rolled off.

"Whoaaa!" I yelped.

Moose let out a deep laugh that shook the basement walls. And then he ended it with a burp.

"Moose, you're disgusting," Mindy groaned.

Moose scratched his dark brown crew cut. "Gee, thanks, Mindy."

"Thanks for what?" she demanded.

"For this." He reached out and snatched the paddle right out of her hand.

Moose swung Mindy's paddle around wildly in the air. He missed a hanging lamp by an inch. "Ready for a real game, Joe?"

He threw the Ping-Pong ball into the air and drew his powerful arm back. *Wham*! The ball rocketed across the room. It bounced off two walls and flew back over the net toward me.

"Foul!" Mindy cried. "That's not allowed."

"Cool!" I exclaimed. I dove for the ball and missed. Moose has an amazing serve.

Moose slammed the ball again. It shot over the net and whacked me in the chest.

Thwock!

"Hey!" I cried. I rubbed the stinging spot.

"Good shot, huh?" He grinned.

"Yeah. But you're supposed to hit the table," I told him.

Moose pumped his fat fists into the air. "Super Moose!" he bellowed. "Strong as a superhero!"

My friend Moose is a pretty wild guy. Mindy says he's a total animal. I think he's just got a lot of enthusiasm.

I served while he was still throwing his arms around.

"Hey! No fair!" he declared. Moose charged the table and clobbered the ball. And flattened it into a tiny white pancake.

I groaned. "That's ball number fifteen for this month," I announced.

I grabbed the little pancake and tossed it into a blue plastic milk crate on the floor. The crate was piled high with dozens of flattened Ping-Pong balls.

"Hey! I think you broke your record!" I declared.

"All right!" Moose exclaimed. He leaped on top of the Ping-Pong table and began jumping up and down. "Super Moose!" he yelled.

"Stop it, you jerk!" Mindy screamed. "You're going to break the table." She covered her face with her hands.

"Super Moose! Super Moose!" he chanted.

The Ping-Pong table swayed. Then it sagged under his weight. He was even starting to get on my nerves now. "Moose, get off! Get off!" I wailed.

"Who's going to make me?" he demanded.

Then we all heard a loud, sharp *craaaaack*.

"You're breaking it!" Mindy shrieked. "Get off!"

Moose scrambled off the table. He lurched toward me, holding his hands straight out like the zombie monster we'd seen in *Killer Zombie from Planet Zero* on TV. "Now I'm going to destroy you!"

Then he hurled himself at me.

As he smashed into me, I staggered back and fell onto the dusty cement floor.

Moose jumped onto my stomach and pinned me down. "Say 'Moose's tomatoes are the best!' " he ordered. He bounced up and down on my chest.

"Moo . . . Moose's," I wheezed. "Tomat . . . I can't . . . breathe . . . really . . . help."

"Say it!" Moose insisted. He place his powerful hands around my neck. And squeezed.

"Ugggggh," I gagged. I couldn't breathe. I couldn't move.

My head rolled to the side.

"Moose!" I heard Mindy shriek. "Let him go! Let him go! What have you done to him?"

3

"M-Miiindy," I moaned.

Moose pulled his hands from my throat and lifted his powerful body off my chest.

"What did you do to him — you big monster?" Mindy shrieked. She knelt down by my side and bent over me. She brushed my hair from my eyes.

"Y-you're a . . . a . . ." I stopped and coughed weakly.

"What, Joe? What is it?" Mindy demanded softly.

"You're a SUCKER!" I exclaimed. And burst out laughing.

Mindy jerked her head back. "You little weasel!"

"Tricked you! Tricked you!" I cheered.

"Way to go, dude!" Moose grinned.

I scrambled to my feet and slapped Moose a high five. "Suc-ker! Suc-ker!" we chanted over and over.

Mindy folded her skinny arms in front of her

and glared at us. "Not funny," she snapped. "I'm never going to believe another word you say! Never!"

"Oh, I'm sooooo scared!" I said. I knocked my knees together. "See? My knees are trembling."

"I'm shaking, too," Moose joined in, wiggling his whole body.

"You guys are totally juvenile," she announced. "I'm out of here."

She slid her hands into the pockets of her white shorts and stomped away. But then she suddenly stopped a few feet from the stairs.

In front of the high basement window.

The window that looked out onto Mr. McCall's front yard.

She stared up through the window's sheer white curtain for a second. She squinted her eyes. Then she cried out, "No! Oh, no!"

"Nice try," I replied, flicking a dust ball from the carpet in her direction. "There's nothing out there. I'm not falling for your lame trick!"

"No! It's Buster!" Mindy cried. "He's next door again!"

"Huh?" I sprinted to the window. And jumped onto a chair. I yanked the filmy curtain aside.

Yes. There sat Buster. In the middle of the vegetable patch that covered Mr. McCall's front yard. "Oh, wow. He's in the garden again," I murmured.

"My garden! He'd better not be!" Moose declared, stomping up behind me. He shoved me off the chair to take a look. "If my dad catches Buster in his vegetables, he'll turn that big mutt into mulch!"

"Come on! Hurry!" Mindy pleaded, tugging on my arm. "We have to get Buster out of there. Right away. Before Moose's dad catches him!"

Moose, Mindy, and I raced upstairs and out the front door. We charged across our front lawn, toward the McCalls' house.

At the edge of our lawn, we leaped across the line of yellow and white petunias that Dad had planted. It separates our yard from the McCalls' garden.

Mindy squeezed her fingernails deep into my arm. "Buster's digging!" she cried. "He's going to destroy — the melons!"

Buster's powerful front paws worked hard. He scraped at the dirt and green plants. Mud and leaves flew everywhere.

"Stop that, Buster!" Mindy pleaded. "Stop that — now!"

Buster kept digging.

Moose glanced at his plastic wristwatch. "You'd better get that dog out of there fast," he warned. "It's almost six o'clock. My dad comes out to water the garden at six sharp."

I'm terrified of Mr. McCall. I admit it. He's so big, he makes Moose look like a shrimp! And he's mean.

14

"Buster, get over here!" I begged. Mindy and I both shouted to the dog.

But Buster ignored our cries.

"Don't just stand there. Why don't you *pull* that dumb mutt out of there?" Moose demanded.

I shook my head. "We can't! He's too big. And stubborn. He won't budge."

I reached under my T-shirt and searched for the shiny metal dog whistle I wear on a cord around my neck. I wear it day and night. Even under my pajamas. It's the only thing Buster will obey.

"It's two minutes to six," Moose warned, checking his watch. "Dad will be out here any second!"

"Blow the whistle, Joe!" Mindy cried.

I brought the whistle up to my mouth. And gave a long, hard blow.

Moose snickered. "That whistle's broken," he said. "It didn't make a sound."

"It's a dog whistle," Mindy replied in a superior tone. "It makes a really high-pitched sound. Dogs can hear them, but people can't. See?"

She pointed to Buster. He had lifted his nose out of the dirt and pricked up his ears.

I blew the whistle again. Buster shook the dirt from his fur.

"Thirty seconds and counting," Moose told us.

I blew the silent dog whistle one more time.

Yes!

Buster came trotting slowly toward us, wagging his stumpy tail.

"Hurry, Buster!" I pleaded. "Hurry!" I held my arms open wide.

"Buster — run — don't trot!" Mindy begged.

Too late.

We heard a loud slam.

Moose's front door flew open.

And Mr. McCall stepped out.

4

"Joe! Come over here. Now!" Moose's dad barked at me.

He lumbered toward his garden, his big belly bouncing in front of him under his blue T-shirt. "Get over here, boy — on the double!"

Mr. McCall is retired from the army. He's used to barking out orders. And having them obeyed.

I obeyed. Buster trotted by my side.

"Was that dog in my garden again?" Mr. McCall demanded, eyeing me coldly. His cold stare could make your blood freeze.

"No, s-sir!" I stammered. Buster settled down beside me with a loud yawn.

I usually don't tell lies. Except to Mindy. But Buster's life was on the line. I had to save Buster. Didn't I?

Mr. McCall bounced up to his vegetable patch. He circled his tomatoes, his corn, his zucchini, his casaba melons. He examined each stalk and leaf carefully.

Oh, wow, I thought. We're in major trouble now.

Finally, he gazed up at us. His eyes narrowed. "If that mutt wasn't in here, why is the dirt all pawed up?"

"Maybe it was the wind?" I replied softly. It was worth a try. Maybe he'd believe it.

Moose stood silently next to me. The only time he's quiet is when his dad is around.

"Um, Mr. McCall," Mindy began. "We'll make sure Buster stays out of your yard. We promise!" Then she smiled her sweetest smile.

Mr. McCall scowled. "All right. But if I catch him even sniffing at my melons, I'm calling the police and having that dog hauled off to the pound. And I mean it."

I gulped. I knew he meant it. Mr. McCall doesn't kid around.

"Moose!" Mr. McCall snapped. "Bring the hose out here and water these casabas! I told you they need to be watered at least five times a day."

"See you later," Moose muttered. He ducked his head and ran toward the back of his house for the hose.

Mr. McCall shot one more dark glance at us. Then he lumbered up his front steps and slammed the door.

"Maybe it was the wind?" Mindy rolled her eyes again. "Wow, that was fast thinking, Joe!" She laughed.

"Oh, yeah? Well, at least I had an answer," I replied. "And remember, it was my whistle that saved Buster. All you did was smile that phony smile."

Mindy and I headed toward our house, arguing all the way. But we stopped when we heard a low moan. A frightening sound. Buster cocked his ears.

"Who's that?" I whispered.

A second later, we found out. Dad lurched around the side of the house, carrying a big watering can.

He was wearing his favorite gardening outfit — sneakers with holes in both toes, baggy plaid shorts, and a red T-shirt that said "I'm All Thumbs in the Garden."

And he was moaning and groaning. Which was really weird. Because Dad is always in an excellent mood when he's gardening. Whistling. Smiling. Cracking lame jokes.

But not today.

Today something was wrong. Really wrong.

"Kids . . . kids," he moaned, staggering toward us. "I've been looking for you."

"Dad — what is it? What's wrong?" Mindy demanded.

Dad clutched his head and swayed from side to side. He took a deep breath. "I-I have something *terrible* to tell you."

5

"What, Dad?" I cried. "Tell us."

Dad spoke in a hoarse whisper. "I found a . . . a fruit fly on our tomatoes! On our biggest tomato. The Red Queen!"

He wiped his sweaty forehead. "How could this happen? I misted. I sprayed. I pruned. Twice this week alone."

Dad shook his head in sorrow. "My poor tomatoes. If that fruit fly ruins my Red Queen, I- I'll have to pull out of the garden show!"

Mindy and I glanced at each other. I knew we were thinking the same thing. The adults around here were getting a little weird.

"Dad, it's only one fruit fly," I pointed out.

"It only takes one, Joe. Just one fruit fly. And our chances for a blue ribbon — destroyed. We have to do something. Right away."

"What about that new bug spray?" I reminded him. "The stuff that came last week from the *Green Thumb* catalog."

20

Dad's eyes lit up. He ran a hand through his flat, rumpled hair. "The *Bug Be Gone!*" he exclaimed.

He jogged up the driveway to the garage. "Come on, kids!" he sang out. "Let's give it a try!" Dad was cheering up.

Mindy and I raced after him.

Dad pulled out three spray cans from a carton in the back of the garage. The words "Wave Bye-Bye to Bugs with *Bug Be Gone!*" were printed on the labels. A drawing showed a tearful bug carrying a suitcase. Waving bye-bye.

Dad handed one can to Mindy and one to me. "Let's get that fruit fly!" he cried, as we headed back to our garden.

We ripped the caps off the cans of *Bug Be Gone.* "One, two, three . . . spray!" Dad commanded.

Dad and I showered the two dozen tomato plants tied to wooden stakes in the middle of the garden.

Mindy hadn't started yet. She was probably reading the ingredients on the can.

"What's all the fuss about?" my mother called, stepping out the back door.

Mom was wearing one of her around-the-house outfits. A pair of Dad's old baggy plaid shorts. And an old blue T-shirt he gave her when he came back from a business trip a few years ago. The T-shirt said "I Mist You!" One of Dad's lame garden jokes.

"Hi, honey," Dad called. "We're about to destroy a fruit fly. Want to watch?"

Mom laughed, crinkling up the corners of her green eyes. "Pretty tempting. But I have to finish a greeting card design."

Mom is a graphic artist. She has an office on the second floor of our house. She can draw the most incredible pictures on her computer. Amazing sunsets, mountains, and flowers.

"Dinner at seven-thirty, everybody. Okay?"

"Sounds good," Dad called as Mom disappeared into the house. "Okay, kids. Let's finish spraying!"

Dad and I showered the tomato plants one more time. We even sprayed the yellow squash plants nearby. Mindy squinted. Aimed the nozzle of her can directly at the Red Queen. And let out a single neat drizzle.

One tiny fruit fly flapped its wings weakly and fell to the ground. Mindy smiled in satisfaction.

"Good work!" Dad exclaimed.

He clapped us both on the back. "I think this calls for a celebration!" he declared. "I have the perfect idea! A quick visit to Lawn Lovely!"

"Oh, nooooo," Mindy and I groaned together.

Lawn Lovely is a store two blocks from our house. It's the place where Dad buys his lawn ornaments. A lot of lawn ornaments.

Dad is as nuts about lawn ornaments as he is about gardening. We have so many lawn ornaments in our front yard, it's impossible to mow the lawn!

What a crowd scene! We have two pink plastic flamingos. A cement angel with huge white wings. A chrome ball on a silver platform. A whole family of plaster skunks. A fountain with two kissing swans. A seal that balances a beach ball on its nose. And a chipped plaster deer.

Weird, huh?

But Dad really loves them. He thinks they're art or something.

And do you know what he does? He dresses them up on holidays. Pilgrim hats for the skunks on Thanksgiving. Pirate costumes for the flamingos on Halloween. Stove-pipe hats and little black beards for the swans on Lincoln's birthday.

Of course, neat and tidy Mindy can't stand the lawn ornaments. Neither can Mom. Every time Dad brings a new one home, Mom threatens to toss it into the garbage.

"Dad, these lawn ornaments are totally embarrassing!" Mindy complained. "People gawk from their cars and take pictures of our front yard. We're a tourist attraction!"

"Oh, please," Dad groaned. "One person took a picture."

That was last Christmas. When Dad dressed all the ornaments as Santa's helpers.

"Yeah. And that picture ended up in the newspaper!" Mindy moaned. "It was soooo embarrassing."

"Well, I think the ornaments are cool," I replied. Someone had to defend poor Dad.

Mindy just wrinkled her nose in disgust.

I know what really bugs Mindy about the ornaments. It's the way Dad sticks them in the yard. Without any order. If Mindy had her way, they would be lined up like her shoes. In nice neat rows.

"Come on, guys," Dad urged, starting down the driveway. "Let's go see if a new shipment of ornaments has come in."

We had no choice.

Mindy and I trudged down the sidewalk after Dad. As we followed him, we thought — no big deal. It's almost dinnertime. We'll just glance over the ornaments at the store. Then we'll go home.

We had no idea we were about to start the most horrifying adventure of our lives.

6

"Can't we drive, Dad?" Mindy complained as the three of us hiked up the steep Summit Avenue hill toward Lawn Lovely. "It's too hot to walk."

"Oh, come on, Mindy. It's only a couple of blocks. And it's good exercise," Dad replied, taking long, brisk strides.

"But it's sooooo hot," Mindy whined. She brushed her bangs away from her face and blotted her forehead with her hand.

Mindy was right. It was hot. But get serious. It was only a two-block walk.

"I'm hotter than you are," I teased. Then I leaned into Mindy and shook my sweaty head at her. "See?"

A few small beads of sweat flew onto Mindy's T-shirt.

"You are so gross!" she shrieked, drawing back. "Dad! Tell him to stop being so disgusting."

"We're almost there," Dad replied. His voice sounded as if he were a million miles away. He

25

was probably dreaming about buying his next lawn ornament.

Just up the block, I spotted the tall, pointy roof of Lawn Lovely. It jutted into the sky, towering over all the houses around it.

What a weird place, I thought. Lawn Lovely is in an old, raggedy three-story house, set back from the street. The whole building is painted pink. Bright pink. The windows are covered with brightly colored shutters. But none of the colors match.

I think that's another reason why Mindy hates this place.

The old house is not in good shape. The wooden floorboards on the front porch are all sagging. And there is a hole in the porch where Mr. McCall fell through last summer.

As we marched past the flagpole in the front yard, I spotted Mrs. Anderson in the driveway. She owns Lawn Lovely. She lives there, too. On the second and third floors.

Mrs. Anderson kneeled over a flock of pink plastic flamingos. She was ripping off their plastic wrap and setting them in crooked rows on her lawn.

Mrs. Anderson reminds me of a flamingo. She's real skinny and wears pink all the time. Even her hair is sort of pink. Like cotton candy.

Lawn ornaments are the only things Mrs. Anderson sells. Plaster squirrels. Kissing angels.

Pink rabbits with wire whiskers. Long green worms wearing little black hats. A whole flock of white geese. She has hundreds of ornaments. Scattered all over her yard. Up the front steps to the porch. And right through the door into the entire first floor of the house.

Mrs. Anderson carefully unwrapped another flamingo and set it down next to a deer. She studied this arrangement, then moved the deer about an inch to the left.

"Hello, Lilah!" my dad called out.

Mrs. Anderson didn't answer. She's a little hard of hearing.

"Hello, Lilah!" Dad repeated, cupping his hands around his mouth like a megaphone.

Mrs. Anderson raised her head from the flamingos. And beamed at my dad. "Jeffrey!" she cried. "How nice to see you."

Mrs. Anderson is always friendly to Dad. Mom says he's her best customer.

Maybe her *only* customer!

"It's nice to see you, too," Dad replied. He rubbed his hands together eagerly and gazed around the lawn.

Mrs. Anderson stuck one last flamingo into the ground. She made her way over to us, wiping her hands on her pink T-shirt.

"Do you have something special in mind today?" she asked my father.

"Our deer is a little lonesome," he explained,

27

shouting so that she could hear him. "I think it needs company."

"Really, Dad. We don't need any more lawn ornaments," Mindy begged. "Mom will be furious."

Mrs. Anderson smiled. "Oh, a Lawn Lovely lawn always has room for one more! Right, Jeffrey?"

"Right!" Dad declared.

Mindy pressed her lips together tightly. She rolled her eyes for the hundredth time that day.

Dad hurried over to a herd of wide-eyed plaster deer, standing in the corner of the yard. We followed him.

The deer stood about four feet tall. White spots dotted their reddish-brown bodies.

Very lifelike. Very boring.

He studied the deer for a few seconds. Then something caught his eye.

Two squat gnomes standing in the middle of the lawn.

"Well, well, what have we here?" Dad murmured, smiling. I could see his eyes light up. He bent down to examine the gnomes.

Mrs. Anderson clapped her hands together. "Jeffrey, you have a wonderful eye for lawn ornaments!" she exclaimed. "I knew you'd appreciate the gnomes! They were carved in Europe. Very fine work."

I stared at the gnomes. They looked like little

old men. They were about three feet tall and very chubby. With piercing red eyes and large pointy ears.

Their mouths curved up in wide, silly grins. And coarse brown hair sprouted from their heads.

Each gnome wore a bright green short-sleeved shirt, brown leggings, and a tall, pointy orange hat. Both wore black belts tied tightly around their chubby waists.

"They're terrific!" Dad gushed. "Oh, kids. Aren't they wonderful?"

"They're okay, Dad," I said.

"*Okay?*" Mindy shouted. "They're *horrible*! They're so gross! They look so . . . so evil. I *hate* them!"

"Hey, you're right, Mindy," I said. "They are pretty gross. They look just like you!"

"Joe, you are the biggest — " Mindy started. But Dad interrupted her.

"We'll take them!" he cried.

"Dad — no!" Mindy howled. "They're hideous! Buy a deer. Buy another flamingo. But not these ugly old gnomes. Look at the awful colors. Look at those evil grins. They're too creepy!"

"Oh, Mindy. Don't be silly. They're perfect!" Dad exclaimed. "We'll have so much fun with them. We'll dress them as ghosts for Halloween. In Santa suits at Christmas. They look just like Santa's elves."

Dad pulled out his credit card. He and Mrs.

Anderson started toward the pink house to complete the sale. "I'll be back in a minute," he called.

"These are the ugliest yet," Mindy groaned, turning to me. "They're completely embarrassing. I'll never be able to bring any of my friends over again."

Then she stomped off toward the sidewalk.

I couldn't take my eyes away from the gnomes. They were kind of ugly. And even though they were smiling, there was something unfriendly about their smiles. Something cold about their glassy red eyes.

"Whoa! Mindy! Look!" I cried. "One of the gnomes just moved!"

Mindy slowly turned to face me.

My wrist was held tightly in the chubby hand. I twisted and squirmed. Tried to tug free.

"Let go!" I squealed. "Let go of me! Mindy — hurry!"

"I — I'm coming!" she cried.

7

Mindy came racing across the yard.

She leaped over the flamingos and sprinted around the deer.

"Hurry!" I moaned, stretching my left arm out toward her. "He's *hurting* me!"

But as my sister came near, her face twisted in fright, I couldn't keep a straight face any longer. I burst out laughing.

"Gotcha! Gotcha!" I shrieked. I danced away from the plaster gnome.

Mindy swung around to slug me. Swung and missed.

"Did you really believe that gnome grabbed me?" I cried. "Are you totally losing it?"

She didn't have time to reply. Dad came jogging down the pink porch steps. "Time to bring our little guys home," he announced, grinning.

He stopped and stared down happily at the ugly gnomes. "But let's name them first." Dad names all of our lawn ornaments.

Mindy let out a loud groan. Dad ignored her.

He patted one of the gnomes on the head. "Let's call this one Hap. Because he looks so happy! I'll carry Hap. You kids take . . ."

He stopped and squinted at the other gnome. There was a small chip on the gnome's front tooth. "Chip. Yep, we'll call this one Chip."

Dad hoisted Hap into his arms. "Whoaaa. He's an armful!" He made his way toward the driveway, staggering under the gnome's weight.

Mindy studied Chip. "You take the feet. I'll grab the top," she ordered. "Come on. One, two, three . . . lift!"

I stooped down and grabbed the gnome by its legs. Its heavy red boot scraped my arm. I let out a cry.

"Quit complaining," Mindy ordered. "At least you don't have this stupid pointy hat sticking in your face."

We struggled down the hill, following Dad.

Mindy and I inched forward, struggling side by side. "Everyone in the neighborhood is gawking at us," Mindy moaned.

They were. Two girls from Mindy's school, wheeling their bikes up the hill, stopped and stared. Then they burst out laughing.

Mindy's pale face grew as red as one of Dad's tomatoes. "I'll never live this down," she grumbled. "Come on, Joe. Walk faster."

I jiggled Chip's legs to make Mindy lose her

grip. But the only thing she lost was her temper. "Quit it, Joe," she snapped. "And hold your end up higher."

As we neared our house, Mr. McCall spotted us trudging up the block. He stopped pruning his shrubs to admire our little parade.

"More lawn ornaments, Jeffrey?" he called out to Dad. I could hear him chuckling.

Mr. McCall is mean to Mindy and me. But he and Dad get along fine. They're always kidding each other about their gardens.

Mrs. McCall poked her head out the front door. "Cute!" she called out, smiling at us from under her white baseball cap. "Come on in, Bill. Your brother is on the phone."

Mr. McCall set his pruning sheers down and went inside.

We lugged Chip past the McCall driveway and followed Dad into our front yard.

"Over here!" Dad instructed as he set Hap down in the far corner of the yard. Next to Deer-lilah. Deer-lilah is the deer. Dad named her after Lilah from Lawn Lovely.

With our last bit of strength, we dragged Chip over to Dad. These gnomes were heavy. They weighed a lot more than our other ornaments.

Mindy and I plopped the gnome down on the grass and collapsed in the dirt next to him.

Whistling happily, Dad set Chip on one side of the deer. And Hap on the other.

He stepped back to study them. "What cheerful little guys!" he declared. "I've got to show your mom. She won't be able to resist them! They're too cute to hate!"

He hurried across the lawn and into the house.

"Yo!" I heard a familiar cry from next door. Moose jogged across his driveway. "I hear you have some ugly new lawn things."

He charged up to the gnomes and stared. "Way ugly," he boomed.

Moose leaned down and stuck his tongue out at Hap. "You want to fight, shrimp?" he asked the little statue. "Take that!" He pretended to punch Hap in his chubby chest.

"Wreck the runt!" I cried.

Moose grabbed the gnome around his waist and gave him a dozen quick punches.

I scrambled to my feet. "I'll wipe that ugly grin off your face!" I yelled at Chip. I closed my hands around the gnome's neck and pretended to choke him.

"Watch this!" Moose shot out a thick leg and karate-kicked Hap in his small pointy hat. The squat figure wobbled.

"Careful! Stop messing around!" Mindy warned. "You're going to break them."

"Okay," I said. "Let's tickle them!"

"Tickle, tickle!" Moose squeaked as he tickled Hap under the armpits.

"You're a riot, Moose," Mindy declared. "A real — "

Moose and I waited for Mindy to finish insulting us. But instead, she pointed to the McCalls' garden and screamed, "Oh, no! Buster!"

Moose and I spun around and spied Buster. In the middle of Mr. McCall's garden, pawing away at the green stalks.

"Buster! No!" I screamed.

I grabbed the dog whistle and raised it to my mouth. But before I could blow, Mr. McCall exploded out of his front door!

"That stupid mutt again!" he shouted, waving his arms wildly. "Get out of here! Shoo!"

Buster whimpered, turned, and trotted back to our yard, head down, stumpy tail between his legs.

Uh-oh, I thought, studying Mr. McCall's angry face. We're in for trouble now.

But before Mr. McCall could start lecturing us, Dad pushed the front door open. "Kids, your mother says that dinner is almost ready."

"Jeffrey, are you deliberately sending that mutt over to ruin my melons?" Mr. McCall called.

Dad grinned. "Buster can't help it," he replied. "He keeps mistaking your melons for golf balls!"

"Are those tomatoes you're growing?" Moose's dad shot back. "Or are they olives?"

"Didn't you see the tomato I rolled into the

house yesterday?" Dad replied. "I had to use a wheelbarrow!"

Buster danced around the yard. I think somehow he knew he had escaped big trouble.

We started for the house. But I stopped when I heard a heavy thud.

I whirled around to discover Hap lying face down in the grass.

Buster busily licked his face.

"Bad dog," Dad scolded. I don't think Dad likes Buster any more than Mr. McCall does. "Did you knock that gnome over? Get away from there!"

"Buster — come here, boy!" I called. But he ignored me and licked at the face more furiously than ever.

I brought my dog whistle to my lips and gave one quick short blow. Buster raised his head, alert to the sound. He forgot about the plaster gnome and trotted over to me.

"Joe, pick Hap up, will you?" Dad demanded, annoyed.

Mindy held onto Buster. I grabbed the gnome by his shoulders and slowly heaved him to his feet. Then I checked for damage.

Legs. Arms. Neck. Everything seemed okay.

I raised my eyes to Hap's face.

And jumped back in surprise.

I blinked a few times. And stared at the gnome again.

"I — I don't believe it!" I murmured.

8

The gnome's smile had vanished.

Its mouth stood open wide, as if trying to scream.

"Hey — !" I choked out.

"What's wrong?" Dad called. "Is it broken?"

"Its smile!" I cried. "Its smile is gone! It looks scared or something!"

Dad jumped down the steps and ran over. Moose and Mr. McCall joined him.

Mindy walked slowly in my direction, with a suspicious scowl on her face. She probably thought I was playing another joke.

"See?" I cried as everyone gathered around me. "It's unbelievable!"

"Ha-ha! Good one, Joe!" Moose burst out. He punched me in the shoulder. "Pretty funny."

"Huh?" I lowered my eyes to the little figure.

Hap's lips were curved up in a grin. The same silly grin he always wore. The terrified expression had disappeared.

37

Dad let out a hearty laugh. "Good acting job, Joe," he said. "You really fooled us all."

"Maybe your son should be an actor," Mr. McCall said, scratching his head.

"He didn't fool me," Mindy bragged. "That one was lame. Really lame."

What had happened? Had I imagined that open mouth?

Mr. McCall turned to Buster. "Listen, Jeffrey," he started. "I'm serious about that dog of yours. If he comes into my garden again . . ."

"If Buster goes over there again, I promise we'll tie him up," Dad replied.

"Aw, Dad," I said. "You know Buster hates to be tied up. He hates it!"

"Sorry, kids," Dad said, turning to go inside. "That's it. Buster gets one more chance."

I bent down to pet Buster's head. "Only one more chance, boy," I whispered in his ear. "Did you hear that? You only get one more chance."

I woke up the next morning and squinted at the clock radio on my night table. Eight A.M. Tuesday. The second day of summer vacation. Excellent!

I threw on my purple-and-white Vikings jersey and my gym shorts and ran downstairs. Time to mow the lawn.

Dad and I had an agreement. If I mowed the lawn once a week all summer, Dad would buy me a new bike.

I knew exactly which model I wanted, too. Twenty-one gears and really fat tires. The coolest mountain bike ever. I'd be able to fly over boulders!

I let myself out the front door and raised my face to the warm morning sun. It felt pretty good. The grass shimmered, still covered with dew.

"Joe!" I heard a loud bellow.

Mr. McCall's bellow. "Get over here!"

Mr. McCall leaned over his vegetable patch. An angry red vein throbbed in his forehead.

Oh, no, I thought as I edged toward him. What now?

"I've had it," he roared. "If you don't tie that dog up, I'm calling the police! I mean it!"

Mr. McCall pointed to the ground. One of his casaba melons lay in the dirt, broken into jagged pieces. Melon seeds were scattered everywhere. And most of the orange fruit had been eaten away.

I opened my mouth, but no sound came out. I didn't know what to say. Lucky for me, Dad showed up just in time. He was on his way to work.

"Is my son giving you some gardening advice, Bill?" he asked.

"No jokes today!" Mr. McCall snapped. He scooped up the broken pieces of melon and shoved them in my dad's face. "See what your wild dog has done! Now I have only four melons left!"

Dad turned to me. His expression grew stern. "I warned you, Joe! I told you to keep the dog in our yard."

"But Buster didn't do this," I protested. "He doesn't even like melons!"

Buster skulked around behind the flamingos. His ears drooped flat against his head. His tail hung low between his legs. He looked really guilty.

"Well, who else could have done it?" Mr. McCall demanded.

Dad shook his head. "Joe, I want you to tie Buster up in the back. Now!"

I saw that I had no choice. No way I could argue.

"Okay, Dad," I mumbled. I shuffled across the lawn and grabbed Buster's collar. I hauled him to the corner of the backyard and sat him next to his red cedar doghouse. "Stay!" I commanded.

I rummaged through the garage until I found a long piece of rope. Then I tied Buster to the tall oak tree next to his doghouse.

Buster whimpered. He really hates being tied up.

"I'm sorry, boy," I whispered. "I know you didn't eat that melon."

Buster pricked up his ears as Dad came around back to make sure I had tied the dog up. "It's just as well that Buster is tied up today," he said. "The painters are starting on the house this afternoon. Buster would only be in their way."

"Painters?" I asked in surprise. Nobody told me that painters were coming. I hate the smell of paint!

Dad nodded. "They're going to paint over that faded yellow," he said, pointing to the house. "We're having the house painted white with black trim."

"Dad, about Buster . . ." I started.

Dad held up a hand to silence me. "I have to get to work. Keep him tied up. We'll talk later." I watched him make his way to the garage.

This is all Mr. McCall's fault, I thought. All of it! After Dad drove away, I stamped angrily into the garage and grabbed the lawn mower. I pushed the mower around the side of the house and into the front yard. Mindy sat on the front steps, reading. I rammed the mower forward.

"I hate Mr. McCall!" I exclaimed. I shoved the mower around a flamingo. I felt like slicing off its skinny legs. "He is such a jerk. I'd like to smash the other four stupid melons!" I cried. "I'd love to wreck them all so Mr. McCall will leave us alone!"

"Joe, get a grip," Mindy called, peering up from her book.

After I finished mowing, I ran into the house and grabbed a large plastic bag for the grass clippings. When I came back out, Moose was sprawled on our lawn. Several brightly colored plastic rings lay scattered on the grass around him.

"Think fast!" he cried. He hurled a blue plastic ring at me. I dropped the bag and leaped for it.

"Nice catch!" he said, scrambling to his feet. "How about a game of ring toss? We'll use the gnomes' pointy hats."

"How about using Mindy's pointy head?" I replied.

"You are so immature," Mindy said. She stood and walked to the door. "I'm going to find some place quiet to read."

Moose handed me a few rings. He flung a purple one toward Hap. The ring slid neatly around the gnome's hat.

"What a throw!" he exclaimed.

I took a ring and spun around like a discus thrower. I tossed two yellow rings at Chip. They slapped against the gnome's fat face and slipped to the grass.

Moose chuckled. "You throw like Mindy. Watch me!" He leaned forward and hurled two rings. They settled neatly around Chip's pointy hat.

"Yes!" Moose cried. He flexed his bulging muscles. "Super Moose rules again!"

We tossed the rest of the rings. Moose beat me. But only by two points — ten to eight.

"Rematch!" I cried. "Let's play again!"

I dashed over to the gnomes and gathered up

the rings. As I pulled a handful fro
I stared into his face.
    And gasped.
    What *was* that?
    A seed.
    An orange seed about half an inch long.
    Stuck between the gnome's fat lips.

9

"Is that a melon seed?" I asked, my voice trembling.

"A what?" Moose stomped up behind me.

"A melon seed," I repeated.

Moose shook his head. He clapped a big hand against my shoulder. "You're seeing things," he declared. "Come on, let's play!"

I pointed to Chip's mouth. "I'm not seeing things. There! Right there! Don't you see it?"

Moose's gaze followed my finger. "Yeah. I see a seed. So what?"

"It's a casaba melon seed, Moose. Like the ones scattered on the ground."

How could a casaba seed find its way into Chip's mouth?

There had to be an explanation. A simple explanation.

I thought hard. I couldn't think of one.

I brushed the seed from the gnome's lips and watched it flutter to the grass.

44

Then I stared at the gnome's grinning face. Into those cold, flat eyes.

And the gnome stared back at me. I shivered in the heat.

How did that seed get there? I wondered. How?

I dreamed about melons that night. I dreamed that a casaba melon grew in our front yard. Grew and grew and grew. Bigger than our house.

Something startled me out of my melon dream. I fumbled for my alarm clock. One A.M.

Then I heard a howl. A low, mournful howl. Outside the house.

I jumped out of bed and hurried to the window. I peered into the shadowy front yard. The lawn ornaments stood in silence.

I heard the howl again. Louder. Longer.

It was Buster. My poor dog. Tied up in the back yard.

I crept out of my room and down the dark hall. The house was quiet. I started down the carpeted stairs.

A step squeaked under my foot. I jumped, startled.

A second later, I heard another creak.

My legs were shaking.

Cool it, Joe, I told myself. It's only the steps.

I tiptoed through the darkened living room and into the kitchen. I heard a low, rustling sound behind me. My heart started to pound.

I whirled around.

Nothing there.

You're hearing things, I told myself.

I stumbled forward in the dark. Closed my hand around the doorknob.

And two powerful hands grabbed me from behind!

10

"Where do you think you're going?"

Mindy!

I breathed a sigh of relief. And yanked myself away from her grasp.

"I'm going for a midnight snack," I whispered, rubbing my neck. "I'm going to eat the rest of Mr. McCall's stupid melons."

I pretended to cram my mouth full and chew. "Yum! Casabas. I need more casabas!"

"Joe! You'd better not!" Mindy whispered in alarm.

"Hey, I'm kidding," I said. "Buster is howling like crazy. I'm going out to calm him down."

Mindy yawned. "If Mom and Dad catch you sneaking out in the middle of the night . . ."

"It'll just take a few minutes." I stepped outside. The damp night air sent a small chill down my back. I gazed up at the starless night sky.

Buster's pitiful howls rose from the back.

"I'm coming," I called in a loud whisper. "It's okay, boy."

Buster's howls dropped to quiet whimpers.

I took a step forward. Something rustled through the grass. I froze in place. And squinted into the darkness. Two small figures scampered by the side of the house. They scraped across the yard and disappeared into the night.

Probably raccoons.

Raccoons?

That's the answer! The raccoons must have eaten Mr. McCall's melon. I wanted to wake up Dad and tell him. But I decided to wait till morning.

I felt much better. That meant that Buster could be set free. I made my way over to Buster and sat next to him on the dew-wet grass.

"Buster," I whispered. "I'm here."

His big brown eyes drooped sadly. I threw my arms around his furry neck. "You won't be tied up for long, Buster," I promised. "You'll see. I'll tell Dad about the raccoons first thing in the morning."

Buster licked my hand gratefully. "And tomorrow I'll take you for a long walk," I whispered. "How's that, boy? Now go to sleep."

I slipped back inside the house and jumped into bed. I felt good. I had solved the mystery of the melon. Our troubles with Mr. McCall were over, I thought.

But I thought wrong.

Our troubles were just beginning.

"I don't believe it! I don't believe it!" Mr. McCall's cries cut through the quiet morning, waking me from my heavy sleep.

I rubbed my eyes and glanced at the clock radio. Six-thirty A.M.

What's all the screaming about?

I hopped out of bed and hurried downstairs, yawning and stretching. Mom, Dad, and Mindy were at the front door, still in pajamas and robes.

"What's happening?" I asked.

"It's Bill!" Dad cried. "Come on!"

We piled outside and stared into our neighbors' garden.

Mr. McCall hung over his vegetable patch in a tattered blue-and-white-checkered robe. He grabbed frantically at his casaba melons, screaming.

Moose and his mother stood behind Mr. McCall in their robes, wide-eyed and silent. Instead of her usual friendly smile, Moose's mom wore a grim frown.

Mr. McCall lifted his head from the garden. "Ruined!" he roared. "They're totally ruined!"

"Oh, boy," Dad muttered. "We'd better get over there, Marion." He started across our front lawn. Mom, Mindy, and I followed.

"Take it easy, Bill," my dad said calmly as he

49

stepped into the McCalls' front yard. "Nothing is worth getting so upset about."

"Easy? Take it easy?" Mr. McCall shrieked. The vein in his forehead throbbed.

The raccoons, I thought. They attacked the casabas again. I've got to tell Dad. Now. Before Buster gets blamed for this, too.

Mr. McCall cradled his four casaba melons in his hands. They were still attached to the vine.

"I came out to water my casabas and I found this . . . this . . ." He was too upset to finish. He held the melons out to us.

"Whoa!" I cried in amazement.

No raccoon could have done this.

No way.

Someone had taken a black marker and drawn big, sloppy smile faces on each melon!

My sister shoved me aside to get a good look.

"Joe!" she shrieked. "That's horrible. How *could* you!"

11

"What are you talking about?" Mr. McCall demanded.

"Yes, Mindy, what *are* you talking about?" Mom asked.

"I caught Joe sneaking outside last night," Mindy replied. "In the middle of the night. He told me he wanted to wreck the rest of the melons."

Everyone turned to stare at me in horror. Even Moose, my best friend. Mr. McCall's face was as red as a tomato again. I saw him clenching and unclenching his fists.

Everyone stared at me in shocked silence. The smile faces on the melons stared at me, too.

"But — but — but — " I sputtered.

Before I could explain, Dad exploded. "Joe, I think you owe us an explanation. What were you doing outside in the middle of the night?"

I felt my face grow red-hot with anger. "I went out to calm Buster down," I insisted. "He was howling. I didn't touch the melons. I would never do anything like that. I was only joking when I told Mindy I wanted to wreck them!"

"Well, this is no joke!" Dad exclaimed angrily. "You are grounded for the week!"

"But, Dad — !" I pleaded. "I didn't draw on those melons!"

"Make that two weeks!" he snapped. "And I think you should mow Mr. McCall's grass and water his garden all month. As an apology."

"Whoa, Jeffrey," Mr. McCall interrupted. "I don't want your son — or your dog — in my garden again. Ever."

He rubbed the casaba melons with his huge fingers, trying to erase the ugly black stains. "I hope this comes off," he muttered. "Because if it doesn't, Jeffrey, I'll sue. Believe me, I will!"

Two hours after the melon disaster, I sprawled on the floor of my room. Grounded. With nothing to do.

I couldn't play with Buster in the yard. Because the painters were outside.

So I stayed in my room and reread all of my *Super Gamma Man* comic books.

I ordered a glob of rubber vomit from the *Joker's Wild* catalog for five dollars. That's most of my weekly allowance. Then I sneaked into Mindy's room and mixed up all the clothes in her closet. No more colors in rainbow order.

When I had finished, it still wasn't even noon.

What a totally boring day, I thought, as I wandered downstairs.

"Hand me the yellow, please," Mindy's voice rang out from the den.

I crept toward the door and peeked in. Mindy and her best friend, Heidi, sat cross-legged on the floor. They were decorating T-shirts with fabric paint.

Heidi is almost as annoying as Mindy. Something is always bothering her. She's too cold. Or too hot. Or her stomach hurts. Or her shoelaces are too tight.

I watched silently as the two girls worked. Heidi drew a silver collar on a large purple cat.

Mindy hunched over in concentration and slowly outlined a large yellow flower.

I leaped into the den. "Boo!" I screamed.

"Yaii!" Heidi shrieked.

Mindy jumped up, smearing a big yellow blotch on her red shorts. "You jerk!" she cried. "See what you made me do!"

She scraped at the paint with her fingernails. "Beat it, Joe," she ordered. "We're busy."

"Well, I'm not," I replied. "Thanks to you, Miss Snitch."

"It was *your* bright idea to draw faces on those melons," she snarled. "Not mine."

"But I didn't do it!" I insisted.

Mindy counted off the evidence on her fingers.

"You were up in the middle of the night. You went out in the yard. And you told me you wanted to wreck the rest of the melons."

"I was joking!" I exclaimed. "Don't you know what a joke is? You should try making one sometime."

Heidi stretched out her arms. "I'm hot," she said. "Why don't we go to the pool? We can finish our shirts later."

Mindy fixed her eyes on me. "Joe, do you want to go with us?" she asked in a sweet voice. "Whoops. I forgot. You're grounded." Then she burst out laughing.

I turned and left the two girls in the den. I have to get out of this house, I thought.

I headed for the kitchen. Mom and the painter huddled together at the counter, checking paint swatches.

"We want the onyx black for the trim. Not the pitch black," she instructed, tapping the swatches. "I think you brought the wrong paint."

I tugged on her sleeve. "Mom. Buster's really bored. Can I take him for a walk?"

"Of course not," she replied quickly. "You're grounded."

"Please," I begged. "Buster needs a walk. And that paint smell is making me sick." I held my stomach and made gagging sounds.

The painter shifted impatiently from foot to foot. "Okay, okay," Mom said. "Take the dog."

"Excellent! Thanks, Mom!" I cried. I darted through the kitchen and into the backyard. "Good news, Buster," I exclaimed. "We're free!"

Buster wagged his stumpy tail. I untied the long rope and clipped a short leash to his collar.

We walked about two miles. All the way down to Buttermilk Pond. That's our favorite stick-chasing spot.

I tossed a fat stick into the water. Buster plunged into the cold pond and fetched it. We did that over and over until it was three o'clock. Time to go home.

On the way back to the house, we stopped at the Creamy Cow. They have the best ice cream in town.

I used the last bit of my allowance to treat us both to double-dip chocolate-chip cookie dough cones. Buster liked the cookie dough, but he left all the chocolate chips on the ground.

After we finished our ice cream, we continued home. Buster pulled at his leash excitedly as we strolled up the driveway. He seemed really happy to be back.

He dragged me into the front yard and sniffed everything. The evergreen bushes. The flamingos. The deer. The gnomes.

The gnomes.

Was something different about the gnomes?

I dropped Buster's leash and bent down for a closer look.

I studied their fat little hands. What were those dark smudges on their fingertips. Dirt?

I rubbed their chubby fingers. But the smudges remained.

No. Not dirt.

I leaned in closer.

Paint. Black paint.

12

Black paint. The same color as the smile faces on Mr. McCall's casabas!

I swallowed hard. What's going on here? I wondered. How could the gnomes' hands be covered in paint?

I've got to show someone, I decided.

Mom! She's in the house. She'll help me figure this out.

As I reached our front door, I heard a scraping sound coming from the McCalls' yard.

"Buster! No!" I shouted.

Buster circled Mr. McCall's vegetable patch, his leash dragging behind him.

I quickly shoved my hand under my T-shirt and yanked out my dog whistle. I blew it hard.

Buster trotted right back to me.

"Good boy!" I cried in relief. I shook my finger in his face. I tried to be stern. "Buster, if you don't want to be tied up, you have to stay out of that garden!"

Buster licked my finger with his long, sticky tongue. Then he turned to lick the gnomes.

I watched Buster slobber all over them.

"Oh, no!" I cried. "Not again!"

Chip's and Hap's mouths gaped wide open. In the same terrified expressions I had seen before. As if they were trying to scream.

I slammed my eyes shut. I opened one slowly.

The terrified expressions remained.

What was going on here? Were the gnomes afraid of Buster? Was I going crazy?

My hands trembled as I quickly tied Buster to the tree. Then I ran into the house to search for Mom.

"Mom! Mom!" I panted breathlessly. I found her upstairs, working in her office. "You've got to come outside! Now!"

Mom whirled around from her computer. "What's wrong?" she demanded.

"It's the gnomes!" I cried. "There's black paint on their hands. And they're not grinning anymore. Come out. You'll see!"

Mom slowly shoved her chair away from the computer. "Joe, if this is another joke . . ."

"Please, Mom. It will just take a second. It's not a joke. Really!"

Mom led the way downstairs. She gazed at the gnomes from the front door.

"See?" I cried, standing behind her. "I told you!

Look at their faces. They look like they're screaming!"

Mom narrowed her eyes. "Joe, give me a break. Why did you get me away from my work? They have the same dumb grins they always have."

"What?" I gasped. I ran outside. I stared at the gnomes.

They stared back at me. Grinning.

"Joe, I really wish you'd stop the dumb gnome jokes," Mom said sharply. "They're not funny. Not funny at all."

"But look at the paint on their fingers!"

"That's just dirt," she said impatiently. "Please, go read a book. Or clean your room. Find something to do. You're driving me crazy!"

I sat down on the grass. Alone. To think.

I thought about the casaba seed on one of the gnome's lips. I remembered the first time their mouths had twisted in horror. That was the first time Buster had licked them.

And now they had paint on their fingers.

It all added up.

The gnomes are alive, I decided.

And they're doing horrible things in the Mc-Calls' garden.

The gnomes? Doing horrible things? I must be losing my mind!

Suddenly, I didn't feel too well. Nothing made any sense.

I stood up to go inside.
And heard whispers.
Gruff whispers. Down at my feet.
"Not funny, Joe," Hap whispered.
"Not funny at all," Chip rasped.

13

Should I tell Mom and Dad what I heard? I wondered as we ate dinner that night.

"How was everyone's day?" Dad asked cheerfully. He spooned some peas onto his dinner plate.

They'll never believe me.

"Heidi and I rode our bikes to the pool," Mindy piped up. She arranged a mound of tuna casserole on her plate into a neat square. Then she flicked a stray pea away. "But she got a cramp in her leg, so we mostly sunbathed."

I have to tell.

"I heard something really weird this afternoon," I burst out. "Really, really weird."

"You interrupted me!" Mindy said sharply. She blotted her mouth carefully with her napkin.

"But this is important!" I exclaimed. I started shredding my napkin nervously. "I was in the front yard. All alone. And I heard whispers."

I made my voice low and gruff. "The voices said, 'Not funny, Joe. Not funny.' I don't know who it

61

was. Nobody was there. I . . . uh . . . think it was the gnomes."

Mom banged her glass of lemonade down on the table. "Enough with these gnome jokes!" she declared. "No one thinks they're funny, Joe."

"But it's true!" I cried, crushing my shredded napking into a ball. "I heard the voices!"

Mindy uttered a scornful laugh. "You are so lame," she said. "Please pass the bread, Dad."

"Sure, honey," Dad replied, handing her the wooden tray of dinner rolls.

And that was the end of that.

After dinner, Dad suggested that we water the tomatoes.

"Okay," I replied with a shrug. Anything to get out of the house.

"Want me to get the *Bug Be Gone*?" I asked as we stepped outside.

"No! No!" he gasped. His face turned ghostly pale.

"What's wrong, Dad? What is it?"

He pointed silently at the tomato patch.

"Ohhh," I moaned. "Oh, no!"

Our beautiful red tomatoes had been crushed, mangled, and maimed — seeds and pulpy red tomato flesh everywhere.

Dad stared openmouthed, his hands balled into fists. "Who would do such a terrible thing?" he sighed.

My heart began to throb. My pulse raced.

I knew the truth. And now everyone would have to believe me.

"The gnomes did it, Dad!" I grabbed the sleeve of his shirt and began tugging him to the front yard. "You'll see. I'll prove it!"

"Joe, let go of me. This is no time for jokes. Don't you realize that we're out of the garden show? We've lost our chance for a blue ribbon! Or any ribbon, for that matter."

"You have to believe me, Dad. Come on." I held tightly onto Dad's sleeve. And I wouldn't let go.

As I dragged him out front, I wondered what we would find.

Blood-red tomato juice smeared all over their ugly faces?

Squishy pulp hanging from their tiny fat fingers?

Hundreds of seeds stuck to their creepy little feet?

We approached the gnomes.

My eyes narrowed on the hideous creatures.

And finally we stood right before them.

And I couldn't believe what we found.

14

Nothing.

No juice.

No pulp.

Not a single seed. Not one.

I searched their bodies. Frantically. From their ugly, grinning faces to their creepy, stubby toes.

No clues. Nothing.

How could I have been wrong? My stomach lurched as I turned to face my dad.

"Dad . . ." I started in a shaky voice.

Dad cut me off with an angry wave of his hand. "There's nothing to see here, Joe," he muttered. "I don't want to hear another word about the gnomes. Understand? Not one!"

His brown eyes flashed with fury. "I know who's responsible for this!" he said bitterly. "And he's not going to get away with it!"

He whirled around and trotted into the back-yard. He scooped up a handful of smashed tomato.

The juice oozed between his fingers as he circled the house and charged next door.

I watched Dad march up the McCalls' steps and jab at the doorbell. He began howling before anyone answered the ring. "Bill! Come out here. Now!"

I crouched behind Dad. I'd never seen him this angry before.

I heard the lock turn. The door swung open. And there stood Mr. McCall. In a white jogging outfit. Holding a half-eaten pork chop in one hand.

"Jeffrey, what are you yelling about? It's difficult to digest with all this noise." He chuckled.

"Well, digest this!" Dad screamed. Then he brought his hand up and hurled the smashed tomatoes.

They splattered against Mr. McCall's white T-shirt and dribbled down his white sweatpants. Some of the mushy pulp landed on his clean white sneakers.

Mr. McCall stared down at his clothes in total disbelief. "Are you nuts?" he bellowed.

"No. You are!" my father shrieked. "How could you do this? For a stupid blue ribbon!"

"What are you talking about?" Mr. McCall shouted.

"Oh, I see. Now you're going to play innocent. You're going to pretend you don't know anything. Well, you're not going to get away with this."

Mr. McCall stomped down the steps and planted himself about an inch away from my dad. He puffed out his broad chest and hung over my father menacingly.

"I didn't touch your lousy tomatoes!" he roared. "You wimp! You probably *bought* your blue-ribbon tomatoes last year."

Dad shook an angry fist in Mr. McCall's glaring face. "My tomatoes were the best at the show! Yours looked like raisins next to mine! And whoever heard of growing casabas in Minnesota, anyway? You're going to be the joke of the garden show!"

My whole body shuddered. They're going to get into a fist fight, I realized. And Mr. McCall will *squash* my dad.

"Joke?" Mr. McCall growled. "You're the joke. You and your sour tomatoes. And those stupid lawn ornaments! Now leave before I really lose control!"

Mr. McCall stomped up to his front door. Then he spun around and said, "I don't want my son hanging around with Joe anymore! Your son probably wrecked your tomatoes. Just as he wrecked my melons!"

He disappeared into the house, slamming the door so hard, the porch shook.

That night I tossed and turned in bed for hours. Faces painted on melons. Crushed tomatoes.

66

Whispering lawn gnomes. I couldn't think of anything else.

It was way after midnight, but I couldn't sleep. The gnomes with their leering smiles danced before my closed eyes.

Those grinning faces. Laughing. Laughing at me.

Suddenly the room felt hot and stuffy. I kicked off the thin sheet that covered my legs. Still too hot.

I jumped out of bed and headed for my window. I threw it wide open. Warm, wet air rushed in.

I rested my arms on the windowsill and peered out into the darkness. It was a foggy night. A thick gray mist swirled over the front yard. Despite the heat, I felt a chill down my back. I had never seen it this foggy before.

The fog shifted slightly. The angel slowly came into view as the fog moved away. Then the seal. The skunks. The swans. A flash of pink — the flamingos.

And there stood the deer.

Alone.

All alone.

The gnomes were gone.

15

"Mom! Dad!" I cried. Racing to their bedroom. "Wake up! Wake up! The gnomes are gone!"

Mom bolted straight up. "What? What's wrong?"

Dad didn't budge.

"It's the gnomes!" I shouted, shaking Dad's shoulder. "Wake up!"

My father opened one eye and squinted up at me. "What time is it?" he mumbled.

"Get up, Dad!" I pleaded.

Mom groaned as she snapped on the light next to her bed. "Joe. It's so late. Why did you wake us up?"

"They're — they're gone!" I stammered. "They disappeared. I'm not kidding. I'm really not."

My parents glanced at each other. Then they glared at me. "Enough!" Mom cried. "We're tired of your jokes. And it's the middle of the night! Get to bed!"

"Right now!" Dad added sternly. "We've had

just about enough of this nonsense. We're going to have a serious talk about this. In the morning."

"But — but — but — " I stammered.

"Go!" Dad shouted.

I backed out of the room slowly, stumbling over someone's slipper.

I should have realized that they wouldn't believe me. But someone had to believe me. Someone had to.

I raced down the dark hall to Mindy's room. As I neared her bed, I could hear the whistling sounds she always makes when she lies on her back. She was fast asleep.

I stared down at her for a moment. Should I wake her? Would *she* believe me?

I patted her on the cheek. "Mindy. Wake up," I whispered.

Nothing.

I called her name again. A little louder.

Her eyes fluttered open. "Joe?" she asked drowsily.

"Get up. Quick!" I whispered. "You have to see this!"

"Have to see what?" she groaned.

"The gnomes. The gnomes have disappeared!" I exclaimed. "I think they ran away! Please, get up. Please."

"The gnomes?" she mumbled.

"Come on, Mindy. Get up," I pleaded. "It's an emergency!"

Mindy's eyes shot wide open. "Emergency? What? What emergency?"

"It's the gnomes. They've really disappeared. You have to come outside with me."

"*That's* the emergency?" she screeched. "Are you crazy? I'm not going anywhere with you. You've totally lost it, Joe. Totally."

"But, Mindy — "

"Quit bugging me. I'm going back to sleep."

Then she closed her eyes and pulled the sheet over her head.

I stood in her dark, silent room.

No one would believe me. No one would come with me. What should I do now? What?

I imagined the gnomes ripping up every last vegetable in our garden. Yanking out the yams and smashing the squash. And for dessert, chomping on the rest of Mr. McCall's casabas!

I knew I had to do something. Fast!

I ran from Mindy's room and raced down the stairs. I jerked the front door open and sprinted outside.

Outside into the murky fog.

Swallowed up inside the thick blanket of mist.

So dark and foggy. I could barely see. I felt as if I were moving through a dark dream. A nightmare of grays and blacks. All shadows. Nothing but shadows.

I inched forward slowly, moving as if I were underwater. The grass felt so wet against my bare feet. But I couldn't even see my own feet through the thick carpet of fog.

Like a dream. Like a heavy, dark dream. So many shifting shadows. So silent. Eerily silent.

I pushed on into the haze. I had lost all sense of direction. Was I heading toward the street?

"Ohhh!" I cried out when something grabbed my ankle.

Frantically, I shook my leg. Tried to break free.

But it held on.

And pulled me down.

Down into the whirling darkness.

A snake.

No. Not a snake. The garden hose. The garden hose that I had forgotten to roll up after watering the lawn that night.

Get a grip, Joe. I told myself. You have to calm down.

I pulled myself up and staggered forward. Squinting hard. Trying to see my way. Shadowy figures seemed to reach for me, bend toward me.

I wanted to turn back. And go inside. And climb into my nice, dry bed.

Yes. That's what I should do, I decided.

I turned slowly.

And heard a shuffling sound. The soft thud of footsteps. Nearby.

I listened closely.

And heard the sounds again. Footsteps as light as the mist.

I was breathing hard now. My heart pounding. My bare feet chilled and wet. The dampness creeping up my legs. My entire body shuddered.

I heard a raspy cackle. A gnome?

I tried to turn. Tried to see it in the billowing blackness.

But it grabbed me from behind. Hard around the waist.

And with a dry, evil laugh, it threw me to the ground!

16

As I hit the wet ground, I heard the low, evil laugh again.

And recognized it.

"Moose?"

"Scared you big time!" he muttered. He helped me to my feet. Even in the fog, I could see the big grin on his face.

"Moose — what are you *doing* out here?" I managed to cry.

"I couldn't sleep. I kept hearing weird sounds. I was staring out into the fog — and I saw you. What are you doing out here, Joe? Causing more trouble?"

I wiped wet blades of grass from my hands. "I haven't been causing the trouble," I told him. "You've got to believe me. Look — the two lawn gnomes — they're gone."

I pointed to the deer. Moose could see that the gnomes weren't standing in their spots.

He stared for a long time. "This is a trick —
right?"

"No. It's for real. I've got to find them."

Moose frowned at me. "What did you do, hide
the ugly little creeps? Where are they? Come on,
tell me!"

"I didn't hide them," I insisted.

"Tell me," he repeated, leaning over me, bring-
ing his face an inch from mine. "Or suffer the Ten
Tortures!"

Moose shoved his huge hands hard against my
chest. I fell back and landed in the wet grass
again. He thumped down on my stomach and
pinned my arms to the ground.

"Tell me!" Moose insisted. "Tell me where they
are!" Then he bounced up and down on top of me.

"Stop!" I gasped. "Stop!"

He stopped because lights flashed on in both of
our houses.

"Oh, wow," I whispered. "We're in major trouble now."

I heard my front door bang open. A second
later, Moose's door opened, too.

We froze. "Keep quiet," I whispered. "Maybe
they won't see us."

"Who's out here?" my father called.

"What's going on, Jeffrey?" I heard Mr. McCall
shout. "What's all the noise out here?"

"I don't know," my dad replied. "I thought
maybe Joe . . ." His voice trailed off.

We're safe, I thought. We're hidden by the fog.

Then I heard a low click. The long, thin beam of a flashlight swept across the yard. It settled on Moose and me.

"Joe!" Dad screamed. "What are you doing out there? Why didn't you answer me?"

"Moose!" Mr. McCall shouted in a deep, angry voice. "Get in here. Move it!"

Moose climbed up and raced into his house.

I hoisted myself up from the grass for the second time that night and slowly made my way inside.

Dad crossed his arms tightly across his chest. "You woke us up twice tonight! And you're outside in the middle of the night again! What's wrong with you?"

"Listen, Dad, I only went outside because the gnomes are missing! Check," I begged. "You'll see!"

My father glared at me with narrowed eyes. "These gnome stories are getting out of hand!" he snapped. "I've had it! Now go upstairs. Before I ground you for the entire summer!"

"Dad, I'm begging you. I've never been so serious in my life. Please look," I pleaded. "Please. Please. Please!" And then I added, "I'll never ask you for anything else again."

I guess that's what convinced him.

"Okay," he said, sighing wearily. "But if this is another joke . . ."

My father stepped over to the living room window and peered out into the swirling fog.

"Please let the gnomes still be gone!" I prayed silently. *"Please let Dad see that I'm telling the truth. Please . . ."*

17

"Joe, you're right!" my father declared. "The gnomes *aren't* out there."

He believed me! Finally! I jumped up and shot a fist into the air. "Yes!" I cheered.

Dad wiped at the moist glass pane with his pajama sleeve and squinted out the window again.

"See, Dad! See!" I cried happily. "I was telling the truth. I wasn't joking."

"Hmmm. Deer-lilah's not there, either," he said softly.

"What?" I gasped, feeling my stomach churn. "No. The deer is there! I saw it!"

"Hold on a minute," Dad murmured. "Ahhh. There she is. She was hidden in the fog. And the gnomes! There they are! They're right there, too. They were hidden in the fog. See?"

I stared out the window. Two pointy hats broke through the mist. The two gnomes stood dark and still, in their places beside the deer.

"Noooooo!" I moaned. "I know they weren't there. I'm not playing tricks, Dad. I'm not!"

"Fog can do funny things," Dad said. "One time I was driving through a real pea soup of a fog. I spotted something strange through the windshield. It was shiny and round and it sort of hovered in the air. *Oh, boy,* I thought. *A UFO!* A flying saucer! I couldn't believe it!"

Dad patted me on the back. "Well, my UFO turned out to be a silver balloon tied to a parking meter. Now, Joe. Back to this gnome problem." Dad's face turned stern. "I don't want to hear any more crazy stories. They're only lawn ornaments. Nothing more. Okay? Not another word. Promise?"

What choice did I have? "Promise," I muttered.

Then I dragged myself up the stairs to bed.

What a horrible day — and night. My father thinks I'm a liar. Our tomatoes are ruined. And Moose isn't allowed to hang out with me anymore.

What *else* could possibly go wrong?

I woke up the following morning with a heavy feeling in my stomach. As if I had swallowed a bowl of cement.

All I could think about were the gnomes.

Those horrible gnomes. They were destroying my summer. They were destroying my life!

Forget about them, Joe, I told myself. Just forget about them.

Anyway, today had to be better than yesterday. It sure couldn't be worse.

I peered out my bedroom window. All traces of the fog had been burned away by a bright yellow sun. Buster slept peacefully in the grass, his long white rope snaking through the garden.

I glanced over at the McCalls' house. Maybe Moose is outside helping his dad in the garden, I thought.

I leaned farther out the window to get a better look.

"Oh, noooo!" I moaned. "No!"

18

Globs of white paint splattered over Mr. McCall's red Jeep!

The roof. The hood. The windows. The whole Jeep covered in paint.

This meant major trouble, I knew.

I pulled on a pair of jeans and yesterday's T-shirt and hurried outside. I found Moose in his driveway, his jaw clenched, shaking his head as he circled the Jeep.

"Unbelievable, huh?" he said, turning to me. "When my dad saw this, he had a cow!"

"Why didn't he park in the garage?" I asked. Mr. McCall always parks the Jeep in their two-car garage.

Moose shrugged. "Mom's been cleaning out the basement and attic for a yard sale. She stuck about a million boxes of junk in the garage. So Dad had to park in the driveway last night."

Moose patted the roof of the Jeep. "The paint is still sticky. Touch it."

I touched it. Sticky.

"My dad is steaming!" Moose declared. "At first he thought your dad did it. You know. Because of the tomatoes. But Mom told him that that was ridiculous. So he called the police. He said he won't rest until whoever did it is thrown in jail!"

"He said *that*?" I asked. My mouth suddenly felt as dry as cotton. "Moose, once the police start to check things out, they're going to blame you and me!"

"Blame us? Are you nuts? Why would they blame us?" he demanded.

"Because we were both outside last night!" I said. "And everybody knows it."

Moose's dark brown eyes flickered with fear. "You're right," he said. "What are we going to do?"

"I don't know," I replied sadly. I paced back and forth in the McCalls' driveway, thinking hard. The asphalt felt warm and sticky on my bare feet.

I moved to the grass. And noticed a line of small white paint spots.

"Hey, what's this?" I cried.

I followed the paint trail across the grass.

Over the petunias.

To the corner of my yard.

The paint drips ended where the gnomes stood, grinning at me.

"I knew it! I knew it!" I cried out. "Moose, come look at this trail. The gnomes splashed your car! And did all the other bad things around here."

"Lawn gnomes?" Moose sputtered. "Joe, give up. No one will believe that. Why don't you give it a rest?"

"Check out the evidence!" I demanded. "The melon seed on the gnome's lips. This trail of white paint. I even found black paint on their fingers. Right after your dad found the smile faces on his casabas!"

"Weird," Moose muttered. "Very weird. But lawn gnomes are lawn gnomes, Joe. They don't run around doing mischief."

"What if we prove they're guilty?" I suggested.

"Excuse me? How would we do that?"

"Catch them in the act," I replied.

"Huh? This is nuts, Joe."

"Come on, Moose. We'll do it tonight. We'll sneak out, hide around the side of the house, and watch them."

Moose shook his head. "No way," he answered. "I'm in big trouble after last night."

"And after the police finish, what kind of trouble will you be in then?"

"Okay. Okay. I'll do it," he muttered. "But I think this whole thing is a big waste of time."

"We're going to trap these gnomes, Moose," I told him. "If it's the last thing we do."

Ahhh!

My alarm clock! It didn't go off!

And now it was nearly midnight. And I was

late. I'd promised to meet Moose outside at eleven-thirty.

I leaped out of bed, still dressed in my jeans and T-shirt. I grabbed my sneakers and ran outside.

No moon. No stars. The front lawn lay blanketed in darkness.

The yard was silent. Too silent.

I glanced around for Moose. No sight of him. He probably went back inside when I didn't show.

What should I do now? Stay out by myself? Or go back to bed?

Something rustled in the bushes. I gasped.

"Joe. Joe. Over here," Moose whispered loudly.

He popped his head out from behind the evergreen shrubs in front of my house. And waved me over.

I slid down next to him.

Moose punched me hard on the arm. "I thought you chickened out."

"No way!" I whispered back. "This was *my* idea!"

"Yeah, your crazy idea," Moose replied. "I can't believe I'm hiding behind a bush. In the middle of the night. Spying on lawn ornaments."

"I know it sounds crazy, but — "

"Shhh. Did you hearing something?" Moose interrupted.

I heard it. A scraping sound.

I reached into the shrub and parted the thick

green branches. The needles clawed at my hands and arms. I jerked my arms out quickly. Too quickly. Blood dripped from my fingers where two needles had pierced right through my skin.

The scraping sound came closer.

My heart pounded in my chest.

Closer.

Moose and I sat there. We exchanged frightened glances.

I had to look. I had to see what was making those sounds.

I parted the needles once again. And stared through the mass of needled branches. Two small, glowing eyes met mine!

"Get it, Moose! Get it!" I cried.

Moose jumped up from behind the bush. Just in time — to see it scamper away.

"A raccoon! It was only a raccoon!"

I let out a long sigh. "Sorry, Moose."

We sat there a while longer. We parted the branches every few minutes to check on the gnomes. My arms were scratched raw from the rough needles.

But the gnomes hadn't budged. They stood grinning into the night in their silly suits and caps.

I groaned. My legs felt stiff and cramped.

Moose checked his watch. "We've been out here for over two hours," he whispered. "Those gnomes aren't going anywhere. I'm going home."

"Wait a little longer," I begged him. "We'll catch them. I know we will."

"You're a pretty good guy," Moose said as he parted the bushes for the millionth time. "So I hate to tell you this, Joe. But you're as crazy as — "

He didn't finish his sentence. His mouth dropped open, and his eyes nearly popped out of his pudgy head.

I peered into the shrubs — in time to see the gnomes come to life. They stretched their arms over their heads. And stroked their chins.

They shook out their legs. And smoothed out their shirts.

"They — they're *moving!*" Moose cried.

Too loudly.

And then I lost my balance and fell. Right into the bush.

They've seen us, I realized.

Now what?

19

"No. Oh, man. No!" Moose whispered. He tugged me to my feet. "They're moving. They're really moving!"

Squinting through the branches, we both stared in horror at Hap and Chip.

The gnomes bent their knees, limbering up. Then they each took one stiff step. Then another.

I was right. They are alive, I thought. Very alive.

And they're coming for Moose and me.

We have to run, I told myself. We have to get *out* of here.

But neither of us could take our eyes off the living lawn gnomes!

The full moon suddenly appeared low over the trees. The front lawn lit as if someone had turned on a spotlight. The stocky figures swung their short, fat arms and began to run. Their pointed hats cut through the air like sharks' fins.

They scrambled toward us on their stumpy legs.

Moose and I dropped to our knees and tried to hide. My whole body was trembling so hard, I was making the bush shake!

The gnomes ran closer. So close that I could see the dark red of their evil eyes and the white gleam of their grins.

I clenched my fists so tightly, my hands ached. What were they going to do to us?

I shut my eyes — and heard them run past. I heard thudding footsteps. Whistling breaths.

I opened my eyes to see them racing across the cement walk and around the side of the house.

"Moose — they didn't see us!" I whispered happily.

We helped each other to our feet. I felt dizzy. The dark ground tilted. My legs felt soft and rubbery like Jell-O.

Moose wiped his sweaty brow. "Where are they going?" he whispered.

I shook my head. "I don't know. But we have to follow them. Come on."

We gave each other a quick thumbs-up and stepped out from our hiding place. I led the way. We moved across the cement walk and past the front porch. Toward the side of the house.

I stopped when I heard their raspy voices, talking low. Just up ahead.

Moose grabbed my shoulder, his eyes wide open in alarm. "I'm getting out of here. Now!"

I turned around. "No!" I pleaded. "You've got

to stay and help me catch them. We have to show our parents what's been going on here."

He heaved a long sigh. It made me feel a little better to know that a big, tough guy like Moose was as frightened as I was. Finally, he nodded. "Okay. Let's go get them."

Keeping in the dark shadow of the house, we made our way around to the back. I saw Buster, sound asleep beside his dog house in the center of the yard.

And then I saw the two lawn gnomes. They were bent over the pile of paint and brushes and drop cloths the painters had left beside the garage.

Moose and I hung back as Hap and Chip picked up two cans of black paint. They pried the cans open with their thick fingers.

Giggling, the two gnomes swung back the open cans, then hurled the black paint at the side of my house. The black paint spattered the fresh white paint, then dripped down in long, thick streaks.

I clapped a hand over my mouth to keep from screaming.

I knew it. I'd know it all along. But no one would believe me. The gnomes were behind all the trouble around here.

The gnomes returned to the pile for more paint. "We've got to stop them," I whispered to Moose. "But how?"

"Let's just tackle them," Moose suggested. "Tackle them from behind and pin them down."

It sounded simple enough. They were little, after all. Smaller than us. "Okay," I whispered, my stomach fluttering. "Then we'll drag them into the house and show my parents."

I took a deep breath and held it. Moose and I started to inch forward.

Closer. Closer.

If only my legs weren't wobbling like rubber bands!

Closer.

And then I saw Moose go down.

He toppled forward — and hit the ground hard, letting out a loud *"Oooof!"*

It took me a second to see that he had tripped over Buster's rope.

He struggled to get to his feet. But the rope had tangled around his ankle.

He reached down with both hands. Gave it a hard tug.

And woke up Buster!

"Rrrrrrowwwwwf! Rrrrrrowwwwwf!" Buster must have seen the gnomes because he started barking his head off.

The gnomes spun around.

And fixed their eyes on us. In the bright moonlight, their faces turned hard and angry.

"Get them!" Chip growled. "Don't let them escape!"

20

"Run!" I screamed.

Moose and I bolted toward the front of the house.

Buster was still barking his head off.

And over the barking, I heard shrill giggles. The gnomes giggled as they chased after us.

Their feet slapped sharply on the grass. I glanced back, saw their stubby legs moving fast, a blur of motion.

I pumped my legs, gasping for breath, and rounded the side of the house.

I could hear the high-pitched giggles of the two gnomes close behind us.

"Help!" Moose cried. "Somebody — help us!"

My mouth hung open. I struggled to breathe. They were gaining on us.

I knew I had to run faster. But my legs suddenly felt as heavy as bricks.

"Hellllp!" Moose called.

I glanced at the house. Why wasn't anyone waking up in there?

We ran around the house and kept running.

Why were Hap and Chip giggling like that?

Because they knew they were going to catch us?

I felt a stab of pain in my side. "Oh, no!" A cramp.

I felt Moose tugging me. "Don't slow down, Joe. Keep going!"

The pain sharpened, like a knife in my side. "Can't run . . ." I choked out.

"Joe — keep going! Don't stop!" Moose cried, frantically pulling my arm.

But I doubled over, holding my side.

It's all over, I thought. They've got me.

And then the front door swung open. The porch light flashed on.

"What's going on out here?" a familiar voice called.

Mindy!

She stepped out, pulling at the belt of her pink bathrobe. I saw her squint into the darkness.

"Mindy!" I called. "Mindy — watch out!"

Too late.

The gnomes grabbed her.

Giggling loudly, they pinned her arms back. Dragged her down the porch steps. Carried her to the street.

21

Mindy thrashed her arms and kicked her legs. But the giggling gnomes had surprising strength.

"Help me!" Mindy called back to Moose and me. "Don't just stand there — help me!"

I swallowed hard. The pain in my side faded.

Moose and I didn't say a word. We just started chasing after them.

They had already carried Mindy to the street. Their feet slapped on the pavement. In the light from the street lamp, I saw Mindy struggling to free herself.

Moose and I hurtled down the driveway. "Put her down!" I shouted breathlessly. "Put my sister down — now!"

More giggles. They scurried past the McCalls' house. Past the next two houses.

Moose and I ran after them, shouting, begging them to stop.

And then — to our shock — they did stop.

In the shadow of a tall hedge, they set Mindy

down. And turned to us. "We mean you no harm," Chip said.

The gnomes' expressions were serious now. Their eyes peered at us through the darkness.

"I don't *believe* this!" Mindy cried, straightening her robe. "This is crazy! Crazy!"

"Tell me about it," I muttered.

"Please listen to us," Hap rasped.

"We mean you no harm," Chip repeated.

"No harm!" Mindy shrieked. "No harm! You just dragged me from my home! You — you — "

"We only wanted to get your attention," Hap said softly.

"Well, you've *got* it!" Mindy exclaimed.

"We mean you no harm," Chip said once again. "Please believe us."

"How *can* we believe you?" I demanded, finally finding my voice. "Look at all the trouble you've caused. You've ruined the gardens! You splashed paint everywhere! You — "

"We can't help it," Hap interrupted.

"We really can't," Chip echoed. "You see, we're Mischief Elves."

"You're *what*?" Mindy cried.

"We're Mischief Elves. We do mischief. That's our mission in life," Hap explained.

"Wherever there is mischief in the world, we're there," Chip added. "Mischief is our job. We can't help ourselves."

He bent down and broke off a chunk of the

93

concrete curb. Then he pulled open the mailbox across from us and shoved the piece of concrete inside.

"See? I can't help myself. I have to do mischief wherever I go."

Hap giggled. "Without us, the world would be a pretty dull place — wouldn't it?"

"It would be a much *better* place," Mindy insisted, crossing her arms in front of her.

Moose still hadn't said a word. He just stood and stared at the two talking lawn gnomes.

Hap and Chip made pouty faces. "Please don't hurt our feelings," Chip rasped. "Our life isn't easy."

"We need your help," Hap added.

"You want us to help you do mischief?" I cried. "No way! You've already gotten me into major trouble."

"No. We need you to help get us our freedom," Chip said solemnly. "Please — listen and believe."

"Listen and believe," Hap echoed.

"We lived in a land far from here," Chip began. "In a forest deep and green. We guarded the mines and protected the trees. We performed our mischief innocently. But we also did a lot of good."

"We were hard-working people," Hap told us, scratching his head. "And we were happy in our forest home."

"But then the mines were closed and the forests

were cut down," Chip continued. "We were captured. Kidnapped. And taken far from home. We were shipped to your country and forced to work as lawn ornaments."

"Slaves," Hap said, shaking his head sadly. "Forced to stand all day and night."

"That's impossible!" Mindy cried. "Don't you get bored? How do you stand so still?"

"We go into a trance," Chip explained. "Time passes without our realizing it. We come out of the trance at night and go about doing our job."

"You mean mischief!" I declared.

They both nodded.

"But we want to be free," Hap continued. "To go where we want. To live where we choose. We want to find another forest where we can live in freedom." Two tiny gnome tears rolled down his fat cheeks.

Chip sighed and raised his eyes to me. "Will you help us?"

"Help you do *what*?" I demanded.

"Help our friends and us escape?" Chip replied.

"There are six others," Hap explained. "They're locked in the basement. At the store where you bought us. We need your help to set them free."

"We can climb into the basement window," his friend continued. "But we are too short to climb back out. And too short to reach the doorknob to let ourselves out through the door."

"Will you help us escape?" Hap pleaded, tugging the bottom of my T-shirt. "You just have to climb down into the basement. Then help our six friends out the basement door."

"Please help us," Chip begged, tears in his eyes. "Then we'll be gone. To a deep forest. And we will never cause you any more mischief."

"That sounds good to me!" Mindy exclaimed.

"So you'll do it?" Hap squealed.

They both began tugging at us, chirping, "Please? Please? Please? Please? Please?"

Moose, Mindy, and I exchanged troubled glances.

What should we do?

22

"Please? Please? Please? Please?"

"Let's help them," Moose said, finally finding his voice.

I turned to Mindy. I didn't usually ask her advice. But she was the oldest. "What do you think?"

Mindy bit her lower lip. "Well, look how much Buster hates to be tied up," she said. "He only wants to be free. I guess everything deserves to be free. Even lawn gnomes."

I turned back to the gnomes. "We'll do it!" I declared. "We'll help you."

"Thank you! Thank you!" Chip cried happily. He threw his arms around Hap. "You don't know what this means to us!"

"Thank you! Thank you! Thank you!" Hap squealed. He leaped into the air and clicked the heels of his boots together. "Hurry! Let's go!"

"Now?" Mindy cried. "It's the middle of the night! Can't we wait until tomorrow?"

"No. Please. Now," Hap insisted.

"In the darkness," Chip added. "While the store is closed. Please. Let's hurry."

"I'm not dressed," Mindy replied. "I really don't think we can go now. I think — "

"If we stay here longer, we'll have to do more mischief," Chip said with a wink.

I sure didn't want that to happen. "Let's do it now!" I agreed.

And so the five of us crept along the dark street and up the steep hill toward Lawn Lovely. Wow, did I feel weird! Here we were, walking around in the middle of the night with a couple of lawn ornaments! About to break into the store and set six more lawn ornaments free!

The old pink house was a strange enough place during the day. But at night, it was totally creepy. All those lawn animals — deer and seals and flamingos — stared at us through the darkness, with blank, lifeless eyes.

Were they alive, too? I wondered.

Hap seemed to read my mind. "They're only for decoration," he sneered. "Nothing more."

The two excited gnomes made their way quickly across the wide lawn and around the side of Mrs. Anderson's house. Moose, Mindy, and I followed behind.

Mindy clutched my arm with an ice-cold hand. My legs still felt wobbly. But my heart was pounding with excitement — not fear.

Hap and Chip pointed to the long, low window

that led down to the basement. I knelt down and peered inside. Total darkness.

"You're sure the other gnomes are down there?" I asked.

"Oh, yes," Chip declared eagerly. "All six. They're waiting for you to rescue them."

"Please hurry," Hap pleaded, shoving me gently to the window. "Before the old woman hears us and wakes up."

I lowered myself to the edge of the open window. And turned back to my sister and Moose.

"We're coming right behind you," Moose whispered.

"Let's rescue them and get *out* of here," Mindy urged.

"Here goes," I said softly.

I crossed my fingers and slid down into the darkness.

23

I bumped over the windowframe and landed on my feet. A few seconds later, I heard Moose and Mindy slide in after me.

I squinted into the blackness that surrounded us. I couldn't see a thing. I licked my dry lips and sniffed the air. A sharp smell, like vinegar, filled the hot, damp basement. Sweat, I thought. Gnome sweat.

I heard a low giggle from outside. Chip and Hap hurtled over the window ledge and thudded to the floor.

"Hey, guys — " I whispered.

But they scampered off into the darkness.

"What's going on here?" Moose demanded.

"We've got to find the light switch," Mindy whispered.

But before we could move, the ceiling lights all flashed on. I blinked in the sudden blaze of brightness.

And then gasped as I stared across the vast basement — at a sea of lawn gnomes!

Not six! Six *hundred*! Row after row of them, jammed against each other, staring at the three of us.

"Whoa!" Moose cried. "It's a mob!"

"Hap and Chip *lied* to us!" I cried.

Their shirts were different colors. But the lawn gnomes all looked exactly alike. They all wore pointed caps and black belts. They all had staring red eyes, wide noses, grinning lips, and large pointy ears.

I was so startled to see so many of the ugly creatures, it took me a while to spot Hap and Chip. Finally, I saw them at the side of the room.

Hap clapped his hands three times.

And three more times. Short, sharp claps that echoed off the basement walls.

And then the crowd of gnomes came to life, stretching and bending, grinning and giggling, chattering in shrill, excited voices.

Mindy grabbed my arm. "We've got to get out of here."

I could barely hear her over the chattering, giggling mob of gnomes. I glanced up at the basement window. It suddenly seemed so high, so far away.

When I turned back, Hap and Chip had moved in front of us. They clapped their hands for attention.

The hundreds of gnomes instantly fell silent.

"We have brought the young humans!" Hap announced, grinning happily.

"We have kept our promise!" Chip declared.

Giggles and cheering.

And then, to my horror, the gnomes began moving forward. Their eyes flashed excitedly. They reached out their stubby arms toward us. The pointed hats bobbed and slid forward, like sharks on the attack.

Mindy, Moose, and I backed up. Backed up to the wall.

The gnomes crowded up against us. Their little hands plucked at my clothes, slapped my face, pulled my hair.

"Stop!" I shrieked. "Get back! Get back!"

"We came to help you!" I heard Mindy scream. "Please — we came to help you escape!"

Loud giggling.

"But we don't *want* to escape!" a grinning gnome declared. "Now that *you're* here, it's going to be so much fun!"

24

Fun?

What did he mean by *fun*?

Hap and Chip pushed their way back to the front and stepped up beside us. They clapped their hands together to silence the giggling, chattering crowd.

The basement instantly turned silent.

"You tricked us!" Mindy screamed at the two gnomes. "You lied to us!"

They giggled in reply and slapped each other's shoulders gleefully.

"I can't believe you fell for our sad story," Hap said, shaking his head.

"We *told* you we're Mischief Gnomes," Chip sneered. "You should have known we were playing mischief!"

"Great joke, guys," I said, forcing a hoarse laugh. "You fooled us. Way to go. So now let us go home, okay?"

"Yeah. Let us go home!" Moose insisted.

The whole room erupted in laughter.

Hap shook his head. "But the mischief has just begun!" he declared.

Cheers and giggles.

Chip turned to the crowd of excited gnomes. "So what shall we do with our lovely prisoners? Any ideas?"

"Let's see if they bounce!" a gnome called from near the back of the room.

"Yeah! Dribble them!"

"A dribbling contest!"

"No — bounce them against the wall. Bounce and catch!"

More cheers.

"No! Fold them into tiny squares! I love it when we fold humans into squares!"

"Yes! A folding contest!" another gnome cried.

"Fold them! Fold them! Fold them!" several gnomes began to chant.

"Tickle them!" a gnome in front suggested.

"Tickle them for hours!"

"Tickle! Tickle! Tickle!"

The room rang out with their excited chants.

"Fold them! Fold them! Fold them!"

"Tickle! Tickle! Tickle!"

"Dribble! Dribble! Dribble! Dribble!"

I turned to Moose. He stared out at the crowd of chanting gnomes, dazed and frightened. His eyes bulged and his chin quivered.

Mindy had her back pressed up against the basement wall. Her blond hair was matted to her forehead. Her hands were jammed into the pockets of her bathrobe.

"What are we going to do?" she asked me, shouting over the excited chants.

Suddenly I had an idea.

I raised my arms high over my head. *"Quiet!"* I screamed.

The room instantly grew silent. Hundreds of red eyes glared at me.

"Let us go!" I demanded. "Or the three of us will scream at the top of our lungs. We will wake up Mrs. Anderson. And she will be down here in a second to rescue us!"

Silence.

Had I frightened them?

No. The gnomes burst into loud, scornful laughter. They slapped each other's shoulders, hooted, and giggled.

"You'll have to do better than that!" Hap grinned up at me. "We all know that Mrs. Anderson can't hear a thing."

"Go ahead and shout," Chip urged. "Shout all you want. We like it when humans shout." He turned to Hap, and the two of them slapped each other's shoulders and fell on the floor, giggling gleefully, kicking their feet in the air.

Over the vast basement, the chants started up again.

"Tickle! Tickle! Tickle!"

"Fold them! Fold them! Fold them!"

"Dribble! Dribble! Dribble!"

With a long sigh, I turned to my frightened sister and friend. "We're doomed," I muttered. "We don't have a chance."

25

"Tug of War! Tug of War!"

A new chant started in the back of the room and swept up toward the front.

"Yes!" Hap and Chip declared happily.

"Excellent mischief!" Hap cried.

"A Tug of War! We'll tug them till they stretch!" Chip shouted.

"Stretch them! Stretch them!"

"Tug of War! Tug of War!"

"Joe — what are we going to do?" I heard Mindy's frightened voice over the enthusiastic chants.

Think, Joe, I urged myself. Think! There has to be a way out of this basement.

But I felt so dazed. The chants rang in my ears. The grinning faces leered up at us. My thoughts were a jumbled mess.

"Stretch them! Stretch them!"

"Fold them! Fold them!"

"Tickle! Tickle! Tickle!"

Suddenly, over the shrill gnome voices, I heard a familiar sound.

A dog's bark.

Buster's bark.

"Buster!" Mindy cried. "I hear him!"

"I — I did too!" I exclaimed, turning and raising my eyes to the window above our heads. "He followed us! He must be right outside!"

I desperately wished Buster could talk. Could run home and tell Mom and Dad that we were in terrible trouble.

But he could only bark. Or . . . could he do more?

I suddenly remembered how frightened Hap and Chip appeared whenever Buster came around. The terrified expressions on their faces.

My heart fluttered with hope. Maybe the gnomes are afraid of dogs. Maybe Buster can scare them into letting us go. Maybe he can even frighten them back into their trance.

I edged closer to my sister, my back pressed against the wall. "Mindy, I think the gnomes are afraid of Buster. If we get him down here, I think he can save us."

We didn't hesitate. All three of us started shouting up to the window. "Buster! Buster! Come here, boy!"

Could he hear us over the chanting gnomes?

Yes!

His big head peered down at us through the window.

"Good boy!" I cried. "Now, come here. Come down here, Buster!"

Buster's mouth opened. His pink tongue drooped from his mouth, and he started to pant.

"Good doggie!" I crooned. "Good doggie — come down here. Fast! Come, boy! Come, Buster!"

Buster poked his head into the window. And yawned.

"Down, Buster!" Mindy ordered. "Come down here, boy!"

He pulled his head out of the window. And settled down on the ground outside. I could see his head resting on his paws.

"No, Buster!" I shrieked, shouting over the chants. "Come, boy! Don't lie down! Come! Buster, come!"

"*Rowf?*" He pushed his head back into the window. Farther. Farther.

"That a boy! Come on!" I pleaded. "A little more . . . a little more. If you come down here, I'll feed you doggie treats five times a day."

Buster cocked his head to the side and sniffed at the damp, sweaty air of the basement.

I held my arms out to the dog. "Please, Buster.

You're our last chance. Please — hurry! Come down here."

To my dismay, Buster pulled his head out of the window.

Turned.

And trotted away.

26

Mindy and Moose let out long, disappointed sighs. "Buster deserted us," Mindy said softly. Her shoulders sagged. Moose dropped to his knees on the floor, shaking his head.

"Trampoline! Trampoline!"

The chant had changed.

Hap grinned up at us. "Maybe we'll use you for trampolines! That would be fun!"

"It's almost time for a vote!" Chip added, rubbing his hands together eagerly.

"Trampoline! Trampoline!"

"Tug of War! Tug of War!"

I held my hands over my ears, trying to block out the sound of their shrill voices.

Silence. Please let me have silence, I thought. Silence.

The word gave me an idea.

Silence. Buster's dog whistle was silent!

Suddenly, I knew how to bring Buster back!

"Mindy!" I cried "The dog whistle! Buster always comes when I blow the dog whistle!"

Mindy raised her head and brightened. "That's right!" she cried. "Hurry, Joe!"

I grabbed for the shiny metal whistle under my T-shirt. It felt slippery with sweat. This has to work, I thought to myself. It has to bring Buster back.

I pulled the whistle out.

"The whistle!" several gnomes shrieked.

The room instantly grew silent.

I raised the whistle to my lips.

"Quick — blow it!" Mindy screeched.

To my surprise, Hap and Chip both dove at me. They leaped up and slapped at the whistle.

The whistle spun out of my hands.

"Noooo!" I cried in despair.

I grabbed frantically for it.

But it rolled and tumbled away, sliding across the basement floor.

27

Mindy, Moose, and I all dove for it.

But the gnomes were quicker.

A gnome in a bright blue shirt raised the whistle, clutched tightly in his little fist. "I've got it!"

"No, you don't!" Moose cried. He leaped at the gnome. Tackled him around the knees.

The gnome let out a *yelp* as he went toppling to the floor.

The dog whistle fell from his hand.

And bounced across the hard floor toward me.

I scooped it up. Started to raise it to my lips.

Three gnomes leaped onto my shoulders, giggling and grunting.

"Noooo!" I uttered a cry as they batted the whistle from my hand. I dropped to the floor, three gnomes on top of me.

I finally shook them off and jumped to my feet. My eyes searched for the whistle.

I saw a bunch of gnomes diving for the floor, scrambling for it. A few feet away, Moose struggled against four or five gnomes who had formed a line to block him. Mindy was battling another group of gnomes, who held her back, their tiny hands around her legs and waist.

And then I saw Hap raise the whistle high.

The gnomes stepped back, clearing a circle around him.

Hap set the whistle in front of him on the floor. Then he raised his foot high.

He was about to crush it!

"Noooooo!" Another long cry escaped my throat. I scrambled over the floor, half-crawling, half-flying.

As Hap's heavy plaster foot came down, I stretched out my hand.

Fumbled for the whistle.

Grabbed it.

Rolled away as the gnome's foot tromped down heavily. It thudded inches from my head.

I sat up. Raised the whistle to my lips.

And blew as hard as I could.

Now what?

Would the whistle work?

Would Buster come running to rescue us?

28

I blew the silent whistle again.

And turned to the window. Buster, where *are* you?

The gnomes must have been asking the same question. Because they froze in place, too. The excited chattering, giggling, and chanting stopped.

The only sound I could hear was my own shallow breathing.

I stared up at the window. A rectangle of blackness. No sign of Buster.

"Hey — !" Moose's cry made me turn around.

"Look at them!" Moose's voice echoed through the silence.

"Look — they all froze!" Mindy declared. She placed both hands on the red cap of a gnome — and pushed the gnome over.

It clattered to the floor. And didn't move. A hunk of plaster.

"I don't get it!" Moose scratched his crew cut.

Still gripping the dog whistle tightly, I moved around the room, examining the frozen gnomes, pushing them over. Enjoying the silence.

"Back in their trance state," Mindy murmured.

"But *how*?" Moose demanded. "Buster never showed up. If they weren't terrified of the dog, why did they all freeze up again?"

I suddenly knew the answer. I raised the whistle and blew it again. "It was the whistle," I explained. "It wasn't Buster. I had it wrong. They were afraid of the whistle. Not the dog."

"Let's get out of here," Mindy said softly. "I never want to see another lawn gnome as long as I live."

"Wait till I tell my parents about this!" Moose declared.

"Whoa!" I cried, grabbing his shoulder. "We can't tell *anyone* about this. No way!"

"Why not?" he demanded.

"Because no one will believe it," I replied.

Moose stared at me for a long moment. "You're right," he agreed finally. "You're definitely right."

Mindy moved to the wall and stared up at the window. "How do we get out of here?"

"I know how," I told her. I picked up Hap and Chip and stood them beneath the window. Then I climbed onto their caps, lifted my hands to the window, and pulled myself up. "Thanks for the boost, guys!" I called down.

They didn't reply.

I hoped they were frozen for good.

Mindy and Moose followed me out. Of course, Buster was waiting for us in the yard. His stubby tail began to wag as soon as I appeared. He came running over and licked my face till I was sopping wet and sticky.

"Sorry, fella. You're a little late," I told him. "You weren't much help — were you!"

He licked me some more. Then he greeted Mindy and Moose.

"Yaaaay! We're out! We're out!" Moose cried. He slapped me so hard on the back, I thought my teeth were going to fly out!

I turned to my sister. "Tickle! Tickle! Tickle!" I chanted.

"Give me a break!" Mindy cried, rolling her eyes for the thousandth time that day.

"Tickle! Tickle! Tickle!" I made tickling motions with my hands and started to chase her down the street.

"Joe — stop it! Don't tickle me! I'm warning you!"

"Tickle! Tickle! Tickle!"

I knew I'd never forget those high-pitched chants. I knew I'd hear them in my dreams for a long, long time.

The next evening, Mindy and I were watching MTV in the den when Dad came home.

"Be nice to your dad," Mom had warned us earlier. "He's very upset that somebody stole his two lawn gnomes."

Yes, the two gnomes were missing when he woke up.

Big surprise.

Mindy and I were so happy, we didn't have a single argument all day.

And now we were happy to see Dad — except that he had a strange expression on his face. "Uh . . . I've brought home a little surprise," he announced, glancing guiltily at Mom.

"*Now* what?" she demanded.

"Come and see." Dad led us out to the front lawn.

The sun was disappearing behind the trees, and the sky was gray. But I could still see clearly what Dad had purchased at Lawn Lovely this time.

An enormous, brown plaster gorilla!

At least eight feet tall, with gigantic black eyes and a bright purple chest. The gorilla had paws the size of baseball mitts and a head as big as a basketball.

"It's the ugliest thing I ever saw!" Mom cried, both hands pressed to her face. "You're not really going to put that horrible monster on our front lawn — are you, dear?"

Anything is better than those lawn gnomes, I thought. Anything is better than lawn gnomes who come alive and do terrible mischief.

I glanced at Mindy. I had a feeling she was thinking the same thing.

"I think it's a beauty, Dad," I said. "It's the best-looking lawn gorilla I ever saw!"

"It's great, Dad," Mindy agreed.

Dad smiled.

Mom turned and hurried back to the house, shaking her head.

I glanced up at the gorilla's enormous purple-and-brown painted face. "Be a good gorilla," I murmured. "Don't be like those awful gnomes."

Then, as I started to turn away, the gorilla winked at me.

Add *more*

Goosebumps

to your collection . . .
A chilling preview of
what's next from
R.L. STINE

A SHOCKER
ON SHOCK STREET

5

Dad pulled right up to the gate, and the guard peered up. He gave Dad a big smile. Then he pressed a button and the gates slowly swung open. Dad drove the car into the tall, white parking garage beside the studio. He parked in the first space next to the entrance. The garage seemed to stretch on forever. But I could see only three or four other cars inside.

"When we open next week, this garage will be jammed!" Dad said. "There will be thousands of people here. I hope."

"And today, we're the only ones!" Marty cried excitedly, jumping out of the car.

"We're so lucky!" I agreed.

A few minutes later, we were standing on the platform outside the main building, facing a wide street, waiting for the tram to take us on the tour. The street led to dozens of white studio buildings, spread out all the way down the hill.

Dad pointed to two enormous buildings as big

as airplane hangars. "Those are the soundstages," he explained. "They film a lot of movie scenes inside those buildings."

"Does the tour go inside them?" Marty demanded. "Where is Shock Street? Where are the monsters? Are they making a movie now? Can we watch them making it?"

"Whoa!" Dad cried. He placed his hands on Marty's shoulders as if to keep him from flying off the ground. I had never seen Marty so totally wired! "Take it easy, fella," Dad warned. "You'll blow a fuse! You won't survive the tour!"

I shook my head. "Maybe we should put him on a leash," I told Dad.

"Arf arf!" Marty barked. Then he snapped his teeth at me, trying to bite me.

I shivered. The fog rolled in from the hills. The air felt damp and cold. The sky darkened.

Two men in business suits came zooming along the street in a golf cart. They were both talking at once. One of them waved to Dad.

"Can we ride in one of those carts?" Marty asked. "Can Erin and I each have our own cart?"

"No way," Dad told him. "You have to take the automated tram. And remember — stay in the tram car. No matter what."

"You mean we can't walk on Shock Street?" Marty whined.

Dad shook his head. "Not allowed. You have to stay on the tram."

blew against us as the tram made its way down the hill. The sky was nearly as dark as night. Some of the white studio buildings were hidden by the fog.

"Stupid gun," Marty muttered, rolling it around in his hands. "Why do we need this plastic gun? I hope the whole tour isn't this babyish."

"I hope you don't complain all afternoon," I told him, frowning. "Do you realize how awesome this is? We're going to see all the great creatures from the *Shocker* movies."

"Think we'll see Shockro?" he asked. Shockro is his favorite. I guess because he's so totally gross.

"Probably," I replied, my eyes on the low buildings we were passing. They all stood dark and empty.

"I want to see Wolf Boy and Wolf Girl," Marty said, counting the monsters off on his fingers. "And . . . the Piranha People, and Captain Sick, The Great Gopher Mutant, and — "

"Wow! Look!" I cried, pounding his shoulder and pointing.

As the tram turned a sharp corner, The Haunted House of Horror loomed darkly in front of us. The roof and its tall stone turrets were hidden by the fog. The rest of the mansion stood gray against the dusky sky.

The tram took us nearer. Tall weeds choked the

front lawn. The weeds bent and swayed in the wind. The gray shingles on the house were chipped and peeling. Pale green light, dim, eerie light, floated out from the tall window in front.

As we rode closer, I could see a rusty iron porch swing — swinging by itself! — on a broken, rotting porch.

"Cool!" I exclaimed.

"It looks a lot smaller than in the movie," Marty grumbled.

"It's exactly the same house!" I cried.

"Then why does it look so much smaller?" he demanded.

What a complainer.

I turned away from him and studied the Haunted House. An iron fence surrounded the place. As we moved around to the side, the rusty gate swung open, squeaking and creaking.

"Look!" I pointed to the dark windows on the second floor. The shutters all flew open at once, then banged shut again.

Lights came on in the windows. Through the window shades, I could see the silhouettes of skeletons hanging, swinging slowly back and forth.

"That's kind of cool," Marty said. "But not too scary." He raised his plastic gun and pretended to shoot at the skeletons.

We circled The Haunted House of Horror once. We could hear screams of terror from inside. The shutters banged again and again. The porch swing continued to creak back and forth, back and forth, as if taken by a ghost.

"Are we going inside or not?" Marty demanded impatiently.

"Sit back and stop complaining," I said sharply. "The ride just started. Don't spoil it for me, okay?"

He stuck his tongue out at me. But he settled back against the seat. We heard a long howl, and then a shrill scream of horror.

The tram made its way silently to the back of the house. A gate swung open and we rolled through it. We moved quickly through the overgrown, weed-choked backyard.

The tram picked up speed. We bounced over the lawn. Up to the back door. A wooden sign above the door read: ABANDON ALL HOPE.

We're going to crash right into the door! I thought. I ducked and raised my hands to shield myself.

But the door creaked open, and we burst inside.

The tram slowed. I lowered my hands and sat up. We were in a dark, dust-covered kitchen. An invisible ghost cackled, an evil laugh. Battered pots and pans covered the wall. As we passed, they clattered to the floor.

The oven door opened and closed by itself. The teapot on the stove started to whistle. Dishes on the shelves rattled. The cackling grew louder.

"This is pretty creepy," I whispered.

"Ooh. Thrills and chills!" Marty replied sarcastically. He crossed his arms in front of him. "Bor-ring!"

"Marty — give me a break." I shoved him away. "You can be a bad sport if you want. But don't ruin it for me."

That seemed to get to him. He muttered, "Sorry," and scooted back next to me.

The tram moved out of the dark kitchen, into an even darker hallway. Paintings of goblins and ugly creatures hung on the hallway walls.

As we approached a closet door, it sprang open — and a shrieking skeleton popped out in front of us, its jaws open, its arms jutting out to grab us.

I screamed. Marty laughed.

The skeleton snapped back into the closet. The tram turned a corner. I saw flickering light up ahead.

We rode into a large, round room. "It's the living room," I whispered to Marty. I raised my eyes to the flickering light and saw a chandelier above our heads, with a dozen burning candles.

The tram stopped beneath it. The chandelier began to shake. Then, with a hiss, the candles all flickered out at once.

The room plunged into darkness.

Then a deep laugh echoed all around us.

I gasped.

"Welcome to my humble home!" a deep voice suddenly boomed.

"Who is that?" I whispered to Marty. "Where is it coming from?"

No reply.

"Hey — Marty?"

I turned to him. "Marty — ?"

He was gone.

About the Author

R.L. STINE is the author of over three dozen best-selling thrillers and mysteries for young people. Recent titles for teenagers include *I Saw You That Night!*, *Call Waiting*, *Halloween Night II*, *The Dead Girlfriend*, and *The Baby-sitter IV*, all published by Scholastic. He is also the author of the *Fear Street* series.

Bob lives in New York City with his wife, Jane, and fifteen-year-old son, Matt.

GET
Goosebumps
by R.L. Stine

☐ BAB47744-7	#22 Ghost Beach	$3.50
☐ BAB47745-5	#23 Return of the Mummy	$3.50
☐ BAB48354-4	#24 Phantom of the Auditorium	$3.50
☐ BAB48355-2	#25 Attack of the Mutant	$3.50
☐ BAB48350-1	#26 My Hairiest Adventure	$3.50
☐ BAB48351-X	#27 A Night in Terror Tower	$3.50
☐ BAB48352-8	#28 The Cuckoo Clock of Doom	$3.50
☐ BAB48347-1	#29 Monster Blood III	$3.50
☐ BAB48348-X	#30 It Came from Beneath the Sink	$3.50
☐ BAB48349-8	#31 Night of the Living Dummy II	$3.50
☐ BAB48344-7	#32 The Barking Ghost	$3.50
☐ BAB48345-5	#33 The Horror at Camp Jellyjam	$3.50
☐ BAB48346-3	#34 Revenge of the Lawn Gnomes	$3.50
☐ BAB48340-4	#35 A Shocker on Shock Street	$3.50

---

me, thrill me, mail me GOOSEBUMPS Now!

Available wherever you buy books, or use this order form. Scholastic Inc., P.O. Box 7502,
2931 East McCarty Street, Jefferson City, MO 65102

Please send me the books I have checked above. I am enclosing $_____ (please add
$2.00 to cover shipping and handling). Send check or money order — no cash or C.O.D.s please.

Name _____ Age _____

Address_____

City_____ State/Zip _____

Please allow four to six weeks for delivery. Offer good in the U.S. only. Sorry, mail orders are not available to
residents of Canada. Prices subject to change.

GB395

Collect the books all summer
and get your own

Goosebumps
Backpack

Be cool when you go back-to-school!

To get your backpack, send FOUR Goosebumps
Proofs-of-Purchase (originals only) and a check or
money order for $5.00 ($7.00 in Canada) for each
backpack ordered, payable to Scholastic Inc.

Goosebumps Proofs-of-Purchase may be found in the following products throughout the
summer, 1995: *#32: The Barking Ghost* (June); *#33: The Horror at Camp Jellyjam* (July); *Give
Yourself Goosebumps: Escape from the Carnival of Horrors* (July); *Goosebumps Collector's Caps
Collecting Kit* (July); *#34: Revenge of the Lawn Gnomes* (August); and *The 1996 Goosebumps
Calendar* (August). Offer good through September 30, 1995 or while supplies last. Allow
8 to 10 weeks for shipment. Offer valid in U.S. and Canada only. U.S residents mail to:
Goosebumps Backpack Distribution Center, P.O. Box 9200, Waltham, MA 02254-9200.
Canadian residents mail to: Scholastic Canada, c/o Iris Ferguson, 123 Newkirk Road.,
Richmond Hill, Ontario L4C3G5. Void where prohibited.

- -

Goosebumps. Summer Backpack Offer

I am ordering _____ GOOSEBUMPS Backpacks. Enclosed is my
payment of $_____ and _____ Proofs-of-Purchase coupons
(originals only). Please send my GOOSEBUMPS Backpack to:

Name_____

Address_____

City_____State_____Zip_____

Child's Signature_____

Parent/Legal Guardian Signature_____

Curly Cash Curly Cash Curly Cash Curly Cash

Goosebumps   *Proof of Purchase*

Curly Cash Curly Cash Curly Cash Curly Cash

GBBC395